ROOTING FOR KIRAN

MEGHAN MONARCH

MEGHAN MONARCH LLC

ROOTING FOR KIRAN: THE MATE-CUTE SERIES BOOK ONE

Book Cover Design: Illustration by Mrsviloart (Victoria López) – mrsviloart.com

Editor: Andrea Halland - Editing by Andrea

ISBN NUMBERS:

Paperback: 979-8-9885232-2-2

Digital: 979-8-9885232-3-9

First Edition: March 2025

DEDICATION

For my fellow single, hyper-independents... I'm rooting for you.

A NOTE TO THE READER

Dear Reader,

Thank you for deciding to give Rooting for Kiran a chance! I hope you love reading it as much as I loved writing it.

That being said, if you are interested in knowing any possible triggers or important reading details, you can find them in the next paragraph, as well as on my website, where you can also find categories and other scaled ratings for each of my works. Protecting yourself as a reader and a human being is important. If you'd rather not read the list, I suggest flipping the page to skip that.

Rooting for Kiran includes: profanity, graphic sex, casual sex, a one-night stand, a dream turned wake-up sex, sex between a human and an alien, alien transformation from humanoid to true alien form, mentions of an alien invasion of the friendly kind, one brief mention of the 2020 COVID outbreak, and one brief mention of watching pornography.

Please read with care and enjoy your journey,
Meghan

PRONUNCIATION GUIDE

CHARACTERS

- **Kiran**: Keer-in (Our MMC's name)

- **Hamal**: Huh-mall (The name of another alien referenced)

KIRAN'S GREENHOUSE INFORMATION

- **Cēd**: Seed (The name of Kiran's greenhouse)

- **Talahecksiya**: Tal-uh-heck-see-ya (A type of plant)

ALIEN BACKGROUND INFORMATION

- **Dyv'i**: Dye-vee (The alien species that invaded Earth)

- **Dyv'iëdus**: Dye-vee-eh-duhs (The Dyv'i planet name)

- **Cēd'oh**: See-doh (Kiran's Dyv'i subspecies)

- **Jëmm'sa**: Gem-suh (Hamal's Dyv'i subspecies)

- **Kahriyht**: Kah-right (Dyv'i version of angels)

PROLOGUE

When aliens touched down on Earth five years ago, there were various reactions from people all over the planet. Some screamed and hid like in the movies, others were curious and open to learning more, while the rest—mostly millennials—weren't fazed one bit and kept going to work like normal fucking human beings.

What we didn't know then that we do now is that these aliens are shapeshifters. Known as the Dyv'i, they walk around in human-like forms until they encounter their mates—and when they find them and fall in love, their mate is the only one who will ever see them in their true form. Sure, some of them fall in love with each other, but they most often fall in love with humans, which is why so many of them wound up traveling here and choosing to stay.

Welcome to Earth in the year 2025, where instead of the coronavirus outbreak five years back, there was an alien invasion of the friendly kind.

In this series, you'll encounter novellas filled with alien romance, out-of-this-world spice, and lots of surprises.

Will your fated mate be from another planet?

CHAPTER ONE

THEA

"Why are we even doing this, Wren? It's the stupidest holiday ever," I whine.

Wren wrestles another bouquet of mixed flowers into her arms and spins toward me. "Just because we don't have partners doesn't mean making Valentine's into Galentine's is stupid. Who doesn't love getting flowers?"

I roll my eyes. "Me... They die eventually, so why even get them? It's a waste of money."

"You're incorrigible. Not all good things last forever. Some are just meant for a moment. Now, lose the 'tude and grab some flowers, damn it."

Without answering, I wander away toward the opposite end of the greenhouse, where the ugliest flowers seem to be. I spot some strange-looking plants in the alien section. Perfect.

Bending closer to one, I scan the label, trying my best to sound out the name. "Tal-a-heck-siya? Talahecksiya?" The plant is green and bumpy, and has one phallic-shaped arm drooping off the lower table it sits atop, extending almost all the way to the floor. Yep. This is the one.

"Can I help you?" a deep voice asks from behind me.

I jump, dropping the plant's penis arm, and spin around. The impact of the arm against the ledge of the table must have been too much, because the green phallus is now lying on the ground between my legs. Who knew it was that fragile?

My eyes widen down at the plant castration I've involuntarily performed. "Shit. I'll pay for that."

An angry throat clearing jolts my attention up, and what I find nearly knocks my knees out from under me.

One of the aliens. A gorgeous one at that. He has smooth, sage-green skin, a straight, yellow-green crew cut with faded sides, tree trunk-sized arms, and emerald-green eyes. He stands at least seven-feet tall. Easy. *Holy shit.*

"It's highly suggested that customers only touch the items they actually *plan* on purchasing."

I move my right foot over to the other side of the penile plant member to meet my left, then squat down to pick up the object and hold it out to him. "I didn't mean to break it. You just startled me."

He tilts his head as he takes the piece, his ginormous, veiny hand softly brushing against mine. "But again, if you hadn't been touching it, this wouldn't have happened. Either look or pick up. No touching."

I hold up my hands in mock surrender. "I got it, okay? I'm sorry. How much do I owe?"

With a sigh, he moves beside me, staring down at the injured plant before lowering to his knees one at a time until he is eye-level with the pot.

The alien places the separated piece directly against where it broke off, and the moment they touch, the tips of his fingers glow a bright, highlighter yellow. Ever so slowly, the pieces fuse back together. When he's done, it looks like nothing even happened.

"What the fuck? If you can do that, why does it matter that I broke it in the first place?"

Gracefully, he gets back to his feet and looks at me with crossed, rippled arms as his face morphs with agitation. "Just because I can fix something doesn't mean it should be treated carelessly. The process is hard on the plant. There's a big possibility this one may not live as long as what's normally expected now."

Warmth spreads through my chest, because there's something about a big, beefy man—even an alien man—caring for greenery and talking about such fragile things with the utmost care that is extremely endearing.

And... Wait... Am I getting turned on? Yep. Mhm. I sure am.

Great. If he's so in tune with plants, is there a possibility he can tell I'm horny for him?

The thought immediately leaves my mind as something crashes into my back, and I'm sent hurtling right into the hunk's chest with astonishing force. His arms wrap around me, holding me against him, and a loud laugh booms behind me.

Fucking Wren.

CHAPTER TWO

KIRAN

A second after chewing out this woman, another with long blonde hair rushes up behind the plant slayer and crashes into her, sending her flying directly into me.

Thankfully, my quick alien reflexes send my arms out and around her, pulling her into my chest so she doesn't fall to the floor—or worse, into more of our precious plants.

Upon impact, the most delicious scent wafts into my nose, and I can't stop my eyes from closing as I breathe it in.

Her arousal. It's intoxicating.

She must feel my cock harden against her, because she plants both of her palms against my chest and pushes herself out of my hold, spinning toward her friend. Her long, chocolate-brown hair fans out with the action.

"Wren, what the hell is wrong with you?" Her gaze dances between her friend and me. "I'm sorry. She has so many issues. Are you okay?" The second question is directed at me.

I clear my throat. "Uh, yeah. I'm fine. Are you?"

"Yes."

The beauty's friend grins up at me sheepishly. "I'm so sorry, sir. My name is Wren. I love your greenhouse."

I reach out and take her delicate hand in mine, noting how small it is. "That's quite alright. The name is Kiran. And thank you. I've worked very hard to make this what it is today."

"This is *your* greenhouse?" my brunette goddess questions.

I nod. "Yes, it issss…" I draw out the *S* as I wait for her to give me her name, slightly nodding my head in small circles to accentuate the prompt.

Her eyebrows scrunch. "Is your head okay?"

Great. I'm making myself look like a moron…

"Yes. I was hoping to get your name, though."

A small smile stretches across her face. "It's Thea. I'm Thea, and you're Kiran."

I fight back an even bigger smile. "That's correct," I confirm. "Are you ladies ready to check out?"

The blonde one—Wren—holds up her array of bouquets. "I am!"

I can't help the chuckle that falls from my lips at her excitement.

Thea spins back toward the plant she broke mere minutes ago, hugs it to her chest, and shrugs. "I said I'd buy it."

Little does she know, that is the only plant of its kind in my store. And there will never be another. I placed that plant here when I opened this shop five years ago, laced with an unnoticeable scent that could only draw in one special person…

The one destined for me…

My mate.

Leading them up to the register, I shoo off the usual cashier, Grayson—a twenty-one-year-old local college student—with a slight tilt of my head. He gets the gist and wanders off to check in with other customers throughout the greenhouse.

"Will this be together? Or separate?"

Wren pipes up first. "Separate."

But Thea speaks quickly after her. "No! Together, please."

"What? Why?" Wren questions.

Thea rips the bouquets from her friend's arms. "Because I only chose one thing, and if we're really doing this Galentine's thing, I need to contribute more than just this phallic-shaped plant that's going in my bedroom. Alright?"

I nearly choke on my spit. She's going to put my mate-trap plant in her bedroom? The one that's an exact replica of my penis? "Galentine's, huh?"

"Yeah." Thea sighs, staring up at me with crystal-blue eyes, like she's silently begging me to rescue her from this heart-holiday hell. "Wren here wants us to make the day special, since we don't have any partners of our own—"

"Yet!" Wren leans over her friend's shoulder. "We don't have partners *yet*, but someday, we might! No reason we can't still celebrate. Wouldn't you agree, Kiran?"

I nod along. "I'd have to agree."

Thea shrugs at our words as she digs through her bag.

Once I have the bouquets bagged up and returned to Wren, I stare down at the Talahecksiya and decide to do something daring. If I want to see Thea again—maybe even have the chance to ask her out—I need to give her a reason to return.

Simultaneously, I rattle off the order total while placing two fingers to the base of the plant, where they then glow a deep red.

"What are you doing to it?" Thea asks with a little concern in her tone.

The credit card machine beeps, and I manage to finish infecting the plant at the same time she pulls her card out. "Just giving it a little extra love to make up for the…injury."

She pauses as she pushes the card back into a slot inside her bag. "Oh. Right. Well, thank you…Kiran."

I smile at both of them, and they start to make their exit. "Thanks for visiting Cēd!"

But they don't look back.

And even though they don't, I know one thing's for sure. I have to convince her to return. Yes. Because the little illness I gave that plant will set in within a week.

I jog after them. "Excuse me!" I call, prompting them to both turn. "Since you purchased a plant from the alien section, I hope you know that I always offer free assistance if anything happens. You're more than welcome to return at any point if something happens to your Talahecksiya."

Thea nods. "Thank you. I'll keep that in mind."

Please do, my mate. Please keep *me* in mind.

CHAPTER THREE

THEA

I don't understand. It's only been five days since we visited the green-house and created our Galentine's bouquets, and every single one of those cut-up flowers is doing way better than the Talahecksiya I purchased. The poor thing is literally dying before my very eyes.

Reviewing the tag's information again, I tick through the list of daily care requirements:

    1. Give one tablespoon of water

    2. Sprinkle a dash of pepper across the soil

    3. Stroke the branch

That last one is the one I struggle with most. I mean, honestly...if I didn't live alone, I could just imagine what it'd look like for a room-mate to come into my room and catch me giving my new plant a handy. What is this even supposed to do?

The greenhouse wouldn't have printed this as a joke, right? Is it really possible for alien plants to require such...*intimate* care?

My hand pulls down on the green penis branch, rubbing across the soft bumps covering its skin. It's soft, yet textured in a way I can't quite put my finger on.

Well, my finger *is* on it, but that's not the point.

I pull my phone from the pocket of my jeans and dial Wren. She answers on the first ring.

"Hey, girl! What's up?"

I glance over at the plant again. "Do you think alien plants can get sick?"

A beat of silence passes on the line before Wren finally answers. "What do you mean?"

"This plant," I start. "It's going pale along the edges. I think it's dying."

"Well, you did mention that Kiran told you the plant might not do as well because you broke off its willy."

I pinch the bridge of my nose. "Its *willy*?"

She chuckles. "Yeah. That's what you get for castrating the poor thing. Are you going to call the greenhouse?"

"Actually, I might just take it there. Hopefully, they can doctor it up."

Wren whistles. "Oooooo! I think you just wanna see that hot alien again. *Oh, Kiran, fix my penis plant! And while you're at it, show me your p—*"

Click.

Nope. No way. Not happening.

Wren is out of her damn mind if she thinks I would ever say something like that to the hot greenhouse owner from another planet.

And yes, I'll admit Kiran's hot, sure. But between working way past closing hours most nights, taking care of a house on my own, and just barely making time for my own family and friends, I have way too much going on in my life to think about a man, let alone an alien one. I can barely handle a plant.

Besides not currently being on the hunt for companionship, I refuse to rely on a man to support me. I'm completely capable of taking the trash out on my own, replacing the air filter when needed, and tending to the yard... So what would I even need one around for?

Cēd is bustling for a Thursday morning. Thankfully, I have time to stop by on my way to work since it's my later morning and the sales meeting I have has been pushed back to ten.

Squeezing through some of the customers, I all but fight my way to the counter, taking my place in line to wait my turn.

"Thea?" someone calls from behind me.

I spin around, puffing out a breath at the sight that greets me.

It's Kiran. All probably seven feet of him, clad in form-fitting khakis and a black henley that really accentuates the sagey hue of his skin while it sticks to every inch of his fit torso.

Even the longer section of hair atop his head is smoothed over with something that makes it stick down as much as his shirt.

Wait. Is that? No. It couldn't be water, could it?

My eyes dart to the floor quickly and back up, and it takes everything in me not to sigh, because I'll be damned...

The man is wet. Like, he got soaked somehow, judging by the puddle of water gathering at his feet. And when I say it looks like he just walked out of a magazine shoot, I fucking mean it. There's a big chance the world's *Sexiest Man Alive* is right here in Michigan. Hurry! Someone call the press!

"Oh, hi," I sputter, waving my pinky, because I fear if I remove one whole hand, I'll send Willy—who I so aptly named after my conversation with Wren this morning—tumbling to the ground.

I move to take a step toward him, but he holds up a finger, silently asking me to wait, so I do. And boy, am I glad I did.

Kiran shakes his head with just enough force that droplets of water soar and fall from the damp strands of hair. And once that part is done, it only gets better.

Next, he whips off the long-sleeved shirt, revealing a white tank that barely contains his filled-out chest, and puts his large, veiny arms on display. One of them has a full sleeve of what seems to be lines of vines covered in thorns. Very fitting for a greenhouse owner.

Rolling the shirt in his hands, he wrings out as much of the water as he can before pulling it back on. I inwardly sigh.

Who said the show had to end?

CHAPTER FOUR

KIRAN

I knew Thea would return eventually. Just like I planned, the Tala-hecksiya is starting to lose its color along the edges. A few more days and that plant might be done for, possibly taking our bond with it.

The moment I'm done ridding myself of as much of the water from the little hose mishap while watering the plants as I can, I look up, catching sight of the way Thea is staring at me.

Her mouth is slightly open, her chest is heaving with heavy breaths, and her eyelids are droopy.

Did she...*like* what she saw? Did I turn her on by drying off?

Human women are so bizarre with what turns them on. Then again, maybe she's ovulating? There was something about that in our Introduction to Earth courses when we landed here in the year 2020.

I can't recall if we are allowed to ask the women that, but I have a strong suspicion I probably shouldn't.

So, instead, I move closer to her. "Is everything okay? You're not returning your plant, are you?"

My words seem to shake her from her stupor, and with a few rushed, hard blinks, her eyes catch onto mine.

"No. Absolutely not. But Willy is sick, and I was hoping one of you could help."

"I'm sorry... Willy?" I ask.

She rolls her lips in while the corners of her mouth fight not to rise. "Uh, yeah... You know"—she points up to the dangling arm—"with the shape and all."

I can't help the laughter that falls from my lips. "Creative and very fitting. So, why do you think that Willy here is sick?"

Thea hands the plant over so she can point at all the pale edges. "He's losing his color. I've been doing every single thing on the daily steps, but something's wrong. I just know it."

Yeah. You're right, sweet girl. There *is* something wrong. You're meant to be mine, and you still don't know it. And once I figure out a way to tell you without scaring you off, I hope you'll accept that fact.

Instead of saying those things to her, I just say, "I see exactly what you're talking about. Good catch. I think I can do something about this."

"Seriously?" The excitement in her voice has me getting twitchy. I love that she's so thrilled about this plant.

With a nod, I lead the way toward a quiet corner with a table I sometimes work at during the day while the other employees attend to the customers and cash registers.

Thea scurries after me, placing both of her hands on the table and looking down at the plant as I work. Her arms push her plump breasts together, and I can't help sneaking a peek at the cleavage almost bursting its way through the V-shaped scoop of her white silk blouse. She must've stopped here on her way to work, which has me wondering what sort of job she has. Something in a nice office, judging by the business attire.

Clearing my throat, I turn my focus back to the Talahecksiya. "Absolutely. It's sort of the bonus for being one of the aliens that can work on plants. I can definitely fix this, but I'll need to keep it for the day."

She steps back and crosses her arms. "All day? For what? I have a job to get to."

I snicker. "I figured, but no worries, you can swing by and grab Willy on your way back home. Is that okay? This sort of healing takes a few hours, and I want to make sure everything goes according to plan."

"Yeah. I—" Thea stops speaking to pull out her phone. "Do you have a business card, or something with your contact information on it, that I can take a photo of to get in touch with you? Just in case I can't make it before closing and need to let you know."

"You're taking this plant parent thing very seriously, huh?"

Thea's brows furrow. "What the hell is that supposed to mean?"

I throw up my hands, quietly chuckling as I try not to look her up and down. "Nothing. It's endearing to see you care so much about Willy that you're almost treating me like a babysitter."

Her eyebrows rise in shock. "Oh my God. I am, aren't I?" One of her delicate hands reaches up to wrap around her forehead. "How embarrassing. I have no idea what's gotten into me. I'm not a plant person."

"Seems like you are to me."

She shakes her head. "No, you don't understand. I've killed several cacti. I think I'm cursed."

My mouth forms a straight line. "Well, that is a tad worrisome, isn't it?"

"Maybe I should return Willy? His likelihood of surviving will definitely increase tenfold by staying with you."

This is not going as planned. She can't return him—*it*. Damn it. Now she has me giving the plant pronouns.

"Now, now. Let's not get carried away. Why don't we start with seeing what I can do? Come by after work to pick it—*him* up, and we'll go from there. 'Kay?"

Thea nods. "Sure. Yeah... Okay. I'll see you later."

CHAPTER FIVE

THEA

Kiran is the hottest man I've ever laid eyes on. There's no denying that, especially with the wetness between my thighs. A trip to the bathroom is a must before I settle down in my desk chair, that's for sure.

I waddle my way through the entrance of the sales company I work for, for some reason fearing that the wetness might somehow drip down my legs and leave a snail trail to follow. Maybe it can be my own little line of crumbs for Kiran to find me.

Wait... No. I can't allow thoughts like those in my head. My mind isn't in the right headspace for a relationship. I'm busy as hell with work. I love my alone time. It's just me and my quiet, quaint, two-bedroom house.

It's been that way for the last few years; ever since I dumped Jake at the age of twenty-eight. That one really shocked the family, but it had to be done. Despite the four years we were together, we didn't fit like I thought we should. I honestly thought I'd marry him, but we just—grew apart. And oddly enough, once the aliens invaded Earth, I made a lot of other life changes besides Jake. Whatever their presence did to our planet—did to me—had me saying, "Fuck it!"

I'm comfortable being a thirty-three-year-old, single, new plant mom. I even read somewhere once that talking to plants helps them thrive, so I'm not alone. Thanks to Willy, I have something to talk to. Besides him and work, I have a very rigid weekend schedule. There's dinner with friends every Friday, house cleaning and work emails on Saturday, brunch with my parents on Sunday morning, and prepping for the upcoming work week after that. This system works for me, so why would I even consider changing it?

Because it's nice to also get some action once in a while, and action is something I haven't gotten from someone other than myself in the last five years...

How has that much time passed? *Holy shit*. I really do need to get laid.

Everyone normally clocks out by five, except for me, especially since we're down one sales associate and have dozens upon dozens of companies to call and try to sell our many kinds of insurance programs to every single day. I was going to try to get out earlier for Kiran's sake, but that didn't happen. I just hope he's still there... I never did get his contact information before I left, and the greenhouse phone number went straight to their after-hours voicemail when I tried calling on the walk out to my car.

That's why it's hard to shut my brain off as I go five over the speed limit to get to the greenhouse. It's already after eight, and I doubt the shop is even open, which means Willy is probably getting the sleepover with Kiran that I wish I was.

But as I pull around the downtown street corner, I'm both surprised and relieved to find the lights on and a truck in the parking lot. Guilt quickly extinguishes those feelings, though, because the sign with the closing time of six seems to grow larger and larger as I pull up closer to the building, like it's taunting me.

Locking up the car, I swear I barely close the door before I'm running—in heels and a skirt—toward the entrance.

"Kiran! I'm here! I'm so sorry!" I yell as I burst through the unlocked door, shutting it behind me to keep out the winter air.

No one answers, but a delicious green-skinned, shirtless male deep inside the greenhouse catches my attention in the section where you can purchase garden and plant supplies like...soil. Yeah, the very soil Kiran is pulling off of a cart that's piled so tall it stands above his towering frame before he gently sets it on another, much neater, already-started pile.

"Fuck. Me. Sideways," I whisper to myself, basically mopping the drool off my chin.

The way his sage-green skin bunches and pulls with his actions has butterflies fluttering in my stomach; not even just there, but more specifically, in my nether regions.

Come to think of it, maybe my vagina is actually the one who whispered that.

Either way, the absolutely scrumptious visual, combined with my overactive, horny imagination, pulls me far away from here until...

"Thea? Are you okay?" Kiran asks, pulling AirPods from his ears, and I jump at his close presence. When did he move? More importantly, when did he finish unloading all of that soil?

I sputter and cough, spit finding its way down the wrong tube. "Uh, yeah. Sorry, I was—"

"Staring?" he interjects, a wicked smirk pulling up at the corner of his mouth.

My eyebrows scrunch as I attempt a lethal scowl. "I was not!"

He crosses his arms, which is the worst thing he could possibly do, because I can't even try to contain the moan that slips from my mouth at the sight of his popping pectorals and buff biceps.

His eyes widen in alarm. "Uh. What was that?"

There are two ways I can shape this. Either I can woman up, grab myself by the tits, and ask Kiran to sleep with me. Or...I can lie and say that I have a slipped disc that is bothering me today.

Luckily, I'm feeling rather brave in these heels. "It was a moan, Kiran."

"Yeah, I got that. But the *why* is what I'd really like to know, sweet girl."

Sweet girl? Holy fuck. I'm such a fan of pet names. If I wasn't already convinced I'd love a one-night stand with this man, I am now.

"How do you feel about one-night stands?" I question.

His chiseled jaw clenches, and the deep emerald of his eyes seems to sparkle with energy. "I've partaken once or twice. Wouldn't mind a third. Why?"

I smile. "Because I'd like to be your third. Your place or mine?"

"Mine," he almost growls.

CHAPTER SIX

KIRAN

Thoughts of the steamy, sexy and worried, second-guessing variety bombard me as I rush around the greenhouse to close down and lock up.

A one-night stand goes against every single thing that tells you how to snag a partner in life. The two other human women I slept with in the past were obviously not my mates. I had been drinking both times and looking for a hookup, but neither of them knew the true me—the alien version—and that form will definitely show up with Thea tonight...

As a species, we decided not to tell the humans that our alien forms only appeared when becoming intimate with our mates. It's something each of us swears secrecy to with our partners, as well, because that fact might be something that scares humans away from pursuing us, and again, many of us Dyv'i males prefer human companionship.

I'd have to find a way to convince her that this was something not to talk about, but how would I do that without revealing she's meant to be with me forever?

If she's up for a one-night stand, I doubt she's looking for commitment right now. I'm desperate for a way to open her up to the idea.

So I'll give her the hookup she's looking for, determined to make it so good that she'll *have* to come back for more.

"Where's Willy? Is he better?" Thea asks, worry lacing her tone.

I grab him from behind the counter and hand him over to her so I can pull my shirt back on. While I know it'll be coming back off very soon, February days in Michigan are still cold.

"He's perfectly fine. Nothing a little alien power couldn't fix." I shoot her a wink as she begins walking beside me.

The lights on her car flash, hurting my pupils.

"I'll just follow you, then?" She pulls her car door open and sets Willy inside before turning her attention back to me.

I stalk over to her, gently close the door, and flatten my body against hers so she's sandwiched between me and her car. Then I box her in by placing both arms on the top of her vehicle and stare down at her. "If I only have one night to fuck you, Thea, you'll be staying the night. You'll get very little sleep, but you'll get many orgasms. Now, lock your car, get your sexy ass in my truck, and let's go. Willy will be fine until tomorrow."

Her throat bobs with a big swallow, and I can't help but lick my lips. Hopefully, I'll get to watch her throat do that again as she gulps down my cum tonight.

"Do I need to run you past your house?"

She shakes her head. "Actually, no. I have an emergency bag in my trunk, just in case."

I follow her around the rear of her car, then reach into the trunk as it opens, rip out the only purple duffle bag inside, slam it closed, and head straight to the truck. I have the bag tossed in the back and the passenger door open before she even has her car locked.

Thea struts over to me, the front of her skirt slightly bunching with her movement. Her arousal has been permeating my nostrils since she entered my shop. And now that I know I'll get to be inside her throughout the night, the scent has taken over my senses.

"Your truck is very, um, tall," she mumbles, her gaze moving between the step and the seat.

I wrap my hands around her waist and lift her, closing my eyes as I breathe in her aroma. "Buckle up," I order.

Halfway through our journey, I notice it's becoming increasingly more difficult for Thea to sit still. Reaching over, I slide my large hand between her strong thighs and spread her legs, pulling a gasp from her.

"Kiran, what are you doing?" Her question drips with attraction. She likes this.

I slowly trail my hand up the inside of her thigh, using my middle finger to pull her panties aside, and thrust my finger into her tight heat. "Fuck." I grunt. "You're soaked, baby."

Thea moans. "That's what you do to me, Kiran. Now, move your finger, please."

It takes extreme effort to keep my eyes on the road, but since the rest of our ride is usually deserted, I quickly peel my other hand from the steering wheel to adjust the rearview mirror so that I can at least catch a glimpse of Thea in the throes of passion I'm providing her.

My left hand back on the wheel and my right hand inside my mate, I begin to pump my finger in and out of her, reaching deeper and deeper every time before I completely turn my hand so my palm is up to the sky and curl my finger to hit that special spot along the inside of her anterior wall.

She throws her hand over her mouth as her moans grow louder and closer together.

"Let me hear you, Thea. You're close, I can feel it. Come for me. Come undone."

Thea erupts with a scream, her walls clamping and spasming around my finger as more wetness drips out of her. Her breathing calms as her body relaxes. "That was..."

"Fucking hot," I finish for her, pulling my hand from her body and sucking her cum from my fingers.

CHAPTER SEVEN

THEA

I literally had to close my eyes so I wouldn't roll into a second orgasm just from watching Kiran suck my essence from his finger. He just gave me the most powerful orgasm of my life, and his dick hasn't even been inside me yet.

I roll my head along the headrest to look at him, my heavy-lidded eyes flitting up and down his torso. This will be my first alien hookup, and I can't wait to tell Wren all about it.

"What's alien sex like?" I wonder aloud, unable to contain the question any longer.

Kiran's dimples catch my attention as he displays a wide grin of blinding-white teeth. "Better than what you've ever experienced with a human, I can tell you that. We have endless endurance, sex organs quite literally designed for the utmost human pleasure, predatory-type attraction to arousal, and completely unique intimate experiences."

I turn my head back to the road. "Why are they completely unique?"

"Well, no two aliens are exactly alike, so that's the first way. And the second one? Hmmm... You'll see."

"That's not ominous or anything." I chuckle. "Is this safe? Am I safe with you? Doing this?"

This time, he chuckles. "Bit late to be asking that, don't ya think?"

My nod is more to myself than him. "Yeah. I messed up there. I don't usually make such rash decisions. Horny me is a different beast entirely."

His head tilts as he pulls into his driveway. "Can't wait to see what that means. But to answer your question, yes, you're safe. I told every single employee at my greenhouse that I was waiting for you to come pick up your plant, my shop is littered with cameras that record footage, we left your car there, and if you didn't already know this, every alien is required to be fit with a governmental tracker. It was part of the agreement when we asked to move to your planet. With the slew of clues we left behind, they could find me in a heartbeat."

"Is that why I've never seen a single news article or broadcast about an alien criminal?"

"Yep. Your species is safe with us. It's sad that you can't be safe with each other," he says.

"Humans suck." I stare up at his house as I answer back. "Your house..." I start before my mouth hangs open, slack-jawed. "It's gorgeous."

Kiran's house is perched atop large tree trunks that are leaning so far down, they almost touch the ground. Sticking out from each trunk are branches of copious lengths and sizes curving up to form a makeshift fence around the perimeter.

The siding seems to be an extremely sturdy tree house type and is covered in vines of various shades of green that somehow remain vibrant despite the freezing temperature and settled snow on the ground.

He grabs my hand and squeezes before we get out and meet in front of the vehicle. "Thank you. It feels like home, as in planetary familiarity."

"That's great, Kiran. I bet it's beautiful there."

He pulls me along behind him as we head for the cut-in steps curving over the trunk that lead straight to the porch. "It is, but not as beautiful as you."

My cheeks heat. His words are incredibly sweet—too sweet for a one-night stand. If we're not careful, attachment could begin, and that's *always* a dangerous game.

So, when he leads me into the house, slips off his boots, and moves to stand beside me after closing the door, I pounce.

Since Kiran is way taller than I am, I focus all my attention on the zipper of his form-fitting jeans, noticing the gigantic bulge that seems as if it just might burst out and jab my eye when freed.

Zipper and button undone, I yank his pants down to his ankles, where he steps out of them as I stand back to admire the dark green lines of tattoo stretching out from the bottom of his boxer briefs and covering both legs. My mouth waters at the sight, and I haven't even had the chance to see him in all his glory yet.

With one hand, I reach down into his briefs and pull out his member. His cock is long, thick, dark green, covered in velvety-soft, yellow-green bumps—and oddly familiar.

"What the fuck?"

Kiran guffaws. "What?"

I look up at him. "Why does your cock resemble Willy?"

His Adam's apple bobs with his swallow before he squats down to wrap his hands under my ass and haul me up against him, where I then wrap my arms and legs around his body and wait for his reply.

"Probably because I'm an alien and Willy is an alien plant." His tone is filled with sarcasm.

I flick his chest. "Jerk. Let's just hope your dick isn't as fragile as Willy. I'd hate for it to fall off before we even start."

He marches us into his room, and I screech as he tosses me on the bed. "Thea, similarities aside, let me show you just how different from Willy I really am."

CHAPTER EIGHT

KIRAN

Sprawled out before me, Thea resembles a kahriyht—my planet's equivalent to Earth's angels. Her dark-brown hair is flared out in waves that stretch across my comforter, the bottom of her blouse has scrunched up with the pull of her large breasts as she lies back, and her skirt has bunched up a few inches, putting her glorious thighs on full display.

She bats her eyelashes. "What are you going to do to me, Kiran?" Thea's sweet voice filters through the air, soaked with a playful, flirtatious tone.

She tries to sit up, but I place my palm on her chest and force her back down before separating her legs and crawling between them.

My bed is custom-made to fit the length of an alien like me with some extra inches available. It's perfect to lie on my stomach and reach her without falling off the end.

I take both sides of her skirt between my fingers and begin pulling it down, her legs closing again, and her underwear partly coming with it. They're a lacy, lime green, and holy shit, I can't wait to see what lies beneath them.

"Just relax, sweet girl," I tell her as she raises her legs and bends her knees so I can finish taking off the skirt and underwear. "Close those eyes and let me make you feel so good."

Thea drops her legs back open and releases a breathy moan that travels straight to my dick. As if it couldn't get any harder, it's now a steel beam barely contained in my boxer briefs.

Focused completely on her bare pussy, I take a deep breath of her aroma and lick my lips. "You smell divine, Thea. Like the perfect meal."

Sensing intimacy with my mate, parts of my body already begin to transform, but I don't want to scare her before making her feel good. At least one orgasm is needed before I can even attempt to try and convince her of being open to sex with me.

The roots running along my tongue push up against the skin, and I can't help the wicked smirk that pulls at the corner of my mouth. She has no idea how much they're going to intensify oral. It will be like nothing she's ever felt before.

I lean in closer, pushing on her inner thighs to spread them farther apart, then tilting them back a bit more so she's fully open to me. Then I flatten my tongue and give her one long, slow, languid stroke from her opening to her already swollen bud.

"Holy fuck, Kiran," she groans. "That feels…"

I place my tongue on her clit and swipe it from right to left so the ridges of the roots bump over it repeatedly.

"SooOooOooo gooOOod." Her syllables grow choppy, just the way I like them.

Leaving my mouth against her mound, I smile so she can feel it. "You like that, baby?"

Thea nods and attempts to lift her head.

"Nuh-uh," I remind her. "Keep those eyes closed and that head flat. Give me another orgasm, and then I'll let you open those breathtaking eyes."

One of her hands reaches up to grasp onto the hair on the back of my head before she pushes me back down, silently ordering me to get back to work. "Then don't stop, bossy pants. We've got a long night ahead of us."

That we do, Thea. That we do…

Her attitude gives me a thrill that I unleash with my mouth. And as I lap up her sweetness, my body continues its transformation, intent to provide my mate with the utmost pleasure.

Two tiny roots pop out from the tip of my tongue, wide enough apart to fit on both sides of her clit, adding just the right amount of extra stimulation as I vibrate my tongue up and down.

Thea twitches and stretches every which way as she blindly absorbs the sensation. Her mewls and moans pick up in speed and volume, showcasing her pleasure. I love that our bodies adjust for the ones we're destined for, because I plan on ruining her for ever looking for anyone else.

She's mine. She will *always* be mine. We are fate.

The scent of her arousal changes, letting me know she's close—very close. That's when she starts gyrating her hips, basically riding my face.

I insert two fingers into her wet heat and curl them up so the pads connect directly with her G-spot and rub in circles over and over and over again until…

My beautiful mate explodes, moisture shooting out and raining down my face. Looks like I've got myself a squirter. *Yum.*

I keep my fingers inside her and my tongue in place, the sounds and words pouring from her luscious lips as she comes down from her high freezing me in place. I'm hesitant to remove any part of myself from her center just yet.

Instead, I slowly and delicately pull my tongue away from her swollen bud and lick up the rest of her moisture. "You taste like...I need *more*," I announce.

"Kiran," Thea breathes out. "That was the most incredible head of my entire fucking life. I'll definitely need you to do that again at some point tonight."

"Anything for you, sweet girl." I stand, towering over her now that I can feel my transformation has completed. "I need you to open your eyes, Thea."

CHAPTER NINE

THEA

There's something about the way Kiran just told me to open my eyes that has fear settling in and my eyes almost gluing themselves shut.

"Why did you say that in that tone?"

"What tone?" he asks.

I cover my eyes with my hands to ensure I don't peek. "Like you're scared of what I'll see?"

Silence settles between us for a moment before he says, "Because I am. Sort of. Keep an open mind? It's sort of an *only-happens-during-sex* thing."

A sputter of laughter escapes my lips. "Kiran, I just got eaten out and finger-fucked to euphoria by an alien. I think my mind—and my legs—are as open as they can get."

But Kiran doesn't laugh like I hoped he would, so rather than drawing this out any longer, I open my eyes...and gasp at what I see.

Kiran has almost completely transformed. Sure, some of his main attributes are still present, proving to me that it is him that stands bare before me, but there are also parts that have changed.

His sage-green skin, yellow-green hair, and emerald-green eyes all remain. But rather than completely smooth skin, his vine-like tattoos I noticed earlier are now raised, and some new ones have even popped up, covering both sides of his face and reaching down over every part of his body like stretches of roadway.

His usually straight hair now has small leaves hanging off the ends of each strand, and tiny twigs are sprinkled throughout the longer hair atop his head.

I finish my assessment by running my eyes back down his body, noticing how some sections of his skin have taken on a stretched, tree bark–like texture. I scan from his amazingly rigid pectorals, over his flexed abs, to the insanely defined V of hip muscles that lead straight to his glorious—

"Wait," I mutter, glancing back up into his eyes. "Your penis. It— Well…"

He rolls those now-glowing emerald eyes. "*Still* looks like Willy, I know. That part is always the same."

Flicking my gaze between his member and his face, I grin. "So, when you said you'd show me how different you are from Willy, you really did mean it. I'm assuming all those raised bumps are going to blow my mind?"

Kiran nods, a close-lipped smile stretching up at the corners of his mouth that showcases his dimples.

"Smile with your teeth," I request. "Please?"

He does, and the flash of white perfection settles me a bit more. As crazy as this is, there are so many small details in this alien form of him that remind me of who I'm really looking at.

Sitting up, I swirl my legs under me to walk on my knees, moving closer to him. "Can you stick out your tongue, too?"

He does, and *damn*. A rippled tongue of, maybe they're roots? Andddddd two smaller roots extending from the tip of his tongue like a rabbit vibrator? That is a major bonus.

"You really are built for top-tier human pleasure, huh?"

His eyes darken as his lids hang heavy, and his smile morphs into a flirty smirk. "For yours, yes."

Isn't that what I just said? Eh. Who the hell cares? I'm about to get epically laid by a ridiculously sexy alien. Let's fucking gooooooo.

"Lie back for me, sweet girl. I want to feel what it's like to have your pussy wrapped around my cock."

Gulp. Dirty talk, check.

I swoop my legs back out in front of me and use my hands to slowly move myself back as Kiran crawls along the bed in my wake. Then I rip off my blouse to toss it on the floor before reaching between my breasts to unlatch my bra.

His hand grabs mine. "Stop," he pleads, and that's when I notice that even the pads of each finger are now rippled with bark-like texture. No wonder he was able to make me squirt for the first time in my entire life. "I'd like to do that, Thea. I want to be the one who frees those perfect tits."

I lie back and smile up at him. "Go for it."

Once Kiran's hands replace mine, he undoes the bra fastener and slowly pulls the cups apart, allowing the fabric to cradle my breasts until they spill out the rest of the way.

"Fuck," he whispers, taking one in each of his strong hands, rubbing the rippled pads of his fingers over my pebbled nipples in a way that has my eyes falling closed again. "Your tits are amazing. So soft, so supple, so..." The bed dips under his movement until I feel his lips replace his fingers on one of my nipples, sucking it into his mouth and then releasing it with a pop. "Delicious," he finishes before sucking it back in.

The pressure has me writhing, my back bowing off the bed to push my breast further into his mouth.

Kiran places a palm over the valley between my breasts and, keeping it flat, adds pressure as that hand travels down over my stomach to my mound. I have a hard time focusing between his mouth and his hand.

He pulls his hand away, and I don't feel it again until he inserts one of his fingers into me, his thumb quickly finding my clit and circling.

I can't help the loud moans falling from my lips as the sensations overwhelm me.

"Kiran!" I call out. "Wait. I want to feel you. Please."

Simultaneously, his hand and his mouth stop moving. His eyes find mine, still glowing bright. "Are you begging for my cock, Thea?"

I nod, batting my lashes up at him.

He smiles at my agreement before sitting back on his knees and moving his gaze down my body. "You're beautiful, Thea. So wet and ready for me."

My body twitches as he inserts two fingers again, collecting my wetness, which he then uses to stroke up and down his hard cock. Holy shit. That's hot...

"Wait... Condom?" I question.

He pauses for a second before moving closer, rubbing the head of his member up and down over my clit, drawing another moan from me. "We won't be needing one of those."

It's hard not to want to pull away from him. "Um, why?"

"Not only is our alien species immune to sexually transmitted infections and diseases, but we also cannot reproduce unless we go into a Dyv'i fertility specialist who would need your approval to have me injected with a serum that reverses the injection we are given at birth that acts as a fault-proof birth control. On our planet, the responsibility of safe sex practices is put on us males, seeing as almost all of the females choose to remain single, some partaking in sexual relations with males for pleasure, rather than reproduction. Very few Dyv'i are destined for each other. Believe it or not, it's a sort of hookup culture there. That's why droves of males relocated here. Our population is an extremely slow-growing breed, so to speak."

Wow. I did not anticipate that answer. Now I can see why a human would want to end up with an alien—no more birth control? Hell yes!

Settling back down as he continues to stroke my clit with his length, I lock eyes with him again. "Then, by all means, fuck me, Kiran."

CHAPTER TEN

THEA

Ever so slowly, Kiran inserts himself into me, inch by aching inch. His thick, textured cock seems to perfectly touch and stroke every centimeter inside of me, making my eyes roll back in my head.

There is no fucking way I'll be able to last long like this.

Kiran moans, and it's a delicious, sweet, torturous sound that speaks directly to each erogenous zone of mine that exists.

I slam a palm to his chest. "Stop."

He does so with a, "What? Why?"

"Can you wait to make those amazing noises until I can acclimate to you a bit? If not, I'm going to come just from hearing them."

Keeping himself buried inside me, he moves his torso up mine until both of his arms box in my head and basically descends into the first part of a push-up. Once he's close enough, he places his mouth directly to my ear. "Do my noises turn you on, sweet girl?" he coos.

With closed eyes, I nod against his mouth so he can feel it, fighting to keep my orgasm at bay. Why do his words seem to speak directly to my pussy? Am I really that worked up from not getting laid in so long?

Something happens inside my vagina. Like, a good thing. Kiran's not moving his body above me, but his penis is working some kind of magic in there. I groan as I feel his cock swell to completely fill me in a way that has all of those bumps I saw earlier grazing and vibrating against my walls.

"Oh, fuck!" I yell. "Yes. Oh, Kiran. That feels so fucking good."

His mouth is still against my ear. "And you expect me to be quiet when your filthy mouth reacts this way to me? To the way my cock pleases you?"

Kiran pulls out a little before pushing back in at a snail's pace, and oh my God, I might only last a minute at this rate. But honestly? Who the fuck cares? We agreed to a night-long sexcapade. I'll have hours to work on my stamina when it comes to him and his sexy mouth.

"So, what do you say, Thea? When can I show you just how good you're making me feel, too?"

"Now," I breathe out.

As Kiran moves back out and in with slow, torturous strokes, my next orgasm begins stirring within me.

"I'm getting close, Kiran. Like, really fucking close."

He releases a big moan, a few beads of sweat that smell like fresh rain dripping down onto my forehead as he brings his mouth to mine.

Our groans mix together at the same time our tongues intertwine. Kiran pumps faster, our kisses grow messy, and the vibrations against my walls intensify.

A scream works its way up my throat. It feels like my skin is going to rip open, like I'm literally about to combust. The feel of his textured tongue against mine only heightens everything.

With a pop that permeates the air, Kiran pulls his lips from mine, and just like in all my masturbation fantasies, words and noises leak from his lips like Peter Piper's instrument drawing my orgasm out. I go feral for a noisy man.

"Fuck, Thea. This pussy—" He gasps. "It was...made for my cock. Uh. Can—" His pumps stop his words for a second. "Can I come inside you?"

"Yes. Please, yes, Kiran."

We erupt. I pulse around him as he spills into me, his cum warm and thick as our chests heave against one another's.

A few minutes pass before Kiran carefully pulls himself out. My orgasm thrums throughout his retreat, and I can't help staring at his powerful chest that continues to heave with his heavy breaths.

But my orgasm doesn't stop. It continues on and on and on...

"Kiran," I moan. "I'm still..." I yelp.

His hands pull my legs and lips apart, and his eyes stare down at where I can feel his release dripping out of me with each spasm. "Coming. Yes, I know, baby. Our ejaculation does that. It has a euphoric property that extends the length of your pleasure. Does it feel good, Thea?"

"Uhhh. I don't know."

He places his fingers just under my opening before pushing them back in. I can tell he's trying to push the cum back inside. "We have to work on that endurance, sweet girl."

I watch as Kiran lowers his head to my mound, his eyes unblinkingly locked on mine. My body shivers when he places a few soft kisses to my skin.

And then his tongue flicks at my clit, making my body convulse in a way that almost has me completing a full sit-up.

"Kiran!" I scream.

I've never had an orgasm go on this long, and I can't tell if it hurts or not.

"It's okay, baby. I've got you. Focus on my tongue as the effects wear off. You're doing such a good job, Thea," he murmurs against my sensitive bud. "There you go."

Closing my eyes, I focus on those delightful licks and flicks instead of the pulsing pressure working its way out of my body.

CHAPTER ELEVEN

KIRAN

The second her body totally relaxed, Thea fell asleep, and I crawled up beside her to take her in my arms.

Now, my body has transformed back into its humanoid form—well, everything besides my dick, since that only changes in size—and I'm curled around her nakedness, running my hand up and down her side while I relish in the softness of her skin, waiting to go another round.

For her first time enduring an orgasm that long, Thea handled it wonderfully. And sex with her? Well, it's everything I've dreamt of since discovering Dyv'i males are destined for a mate; whether or not the latter agrees to the partnership decides the fate of our love life. But finding her here on Earth? It's the whole reason so many of us came here. Besides the large number of hyper-independent, single women of our species, many of them also desire celibacy.

With so few females to mate with us, it's no wonder our population grows at a snail's pace. When the mate search rituals for so many of us didn't work after some time, tons of us relocated to Earth in droves, desperate to find those who are meant for us and feeling a pull to a new planet.

Now I realize that Thea was the one drawing me here, and as I breathe in her scent and close my eyes, I find myself wondering what the odds are of winding up in the same town as her and finally discovering she really and truly exists.

Holy shit.

Thea's lips are wrapped tightly around my cock. She slowly moves up and down my shaft before releasing it with a pop.

She gazes up at me with half-lidded eyes, a smirk pulling up at the corner of her mouth as she lowers her head so her mouth lines up with the base of my shaft.

Then she flattens her tongue to the underside of my dick and licks all the way to the tip before blowing a gentle breath of air back down, cooling where the line of her saliva is. I shiver.

To warm my skin, she kisses her way back up to the tip and—

My eyes slam open wide, my dream feeling way too real for having Thea right next to... *Oh...* I feel her.

Her mouth really is on me, seemingly doing all those things in my dream to wake me up.

I let out a long groan, placing my hand on the back of her head and carefully pushing myself further into her mouth.

"Yes, sweet girl. You take me so well." I get in a few more thrusts before adding, "This is the best wake-up call."

She moans, the vibrations nearly doing me in. I give her hair a delicate yank, a silent plea to pull away for a second.

"What, Kiran?" Her words come out in a breathy moan as her devilish eyes stare up into mine. "Do you want me to stop?" Thea gives me another long lick, and I have to close my eyes to keep control for a second before leveling her with another stare.

I shoot her a wink. "Never, baby. Just wanted to ask if you're okay with me coming in your mouth or not."

Thea's bright blues widen. "Will it send me into another fifteen-minute-long orgasm? I don't know if I'm ready for that again." She chuckles nervously.

"No. It won't do that," I assure her. "Actually, I and my fellow foliage-kind from my planet have very sweet cum. You'll probably enjoy the taste, which will make it much more pleasant for you."

The entire time I talk, Thea works me over with her hand, somehow still keeping me teetering on the edge. How my words come out as calmly as they are beats me.

"Then, by all means, fill my mouth, babe," she whispers against my dick.

An animalistic energy takes over Thea as she all but eats me whole, and within minutes, I'm fisting the sheets and bucking up into her mouth as my climax slides down her throat.

The way her throat bobs while she swallows my cum has my eyebrows involuntarily sliding up toward my hairline, and the way she licks her lips to collect any remaining droplets has me pulling her back up my body and slamming her back down on my cock.

"I'm not done with you yet, sweet girl," I tell her.

We repeat the process off and on throughout the night, bringing one another to multiple orgasms and exploring each other's bodies.

If only there was a way to stop time so I could stay buried within her for eternity, right where I belong.

CHAPTER TWELVE

THEA

Morning comes awfully quick for a night of passion like the one Kiran and I just shared. After I use Kiran's bathroom to shower and get ready—alone, to ensure I'm not made late by his sexy shenanigans—I wander out and find him leaning back against the counter with a cup of coffee in one hand while the other rests atop the marble surface.

Of course, he's shirtless and donning gray sweatpants that leave nothing to the imagination.

"Last night didn't cure you of your boner problem?" I tease.

He sexy-grins into his mug, showcasing his million-dollar smile of straight, white teeth. "I don't think it can be cured when you're around."

I roll my eyes. "Puh-lease, I'm sure you've had similar or better."

"I haven't." Kiran's tone is serious and flat when he answers. "But I probably won't be able to convince you of that. If you decide to keep coming arou—"

My hand flies straight up in the air, halting his words. "One-night stand, Kiran. Remember? That's what we agreed to. I've got way too much going on for a relationship."

"I'm busy, too, Thea. Doesn't mean we can't even attempt to pursue something."

"No," I reply. "Please, don't try to pressure me about this."

He playfully shrugs. "Okay, okay. No peer pressure, got it. I've heard about that *DARE* class you all take in school growing up."

Walking closer to him, I set my bag on the floor and lean on the island to face him. "Are you saying you're like a drug, Kiran?"

His towering frame spins toward the coffee maker, where he pours some of the steaming liquid into a to-go cup that he then offers to me. "Me? Nah. But what we shared last night? Whatever that was is definitely addictive. I'm not sure I'll even be able to give myself a good enough hand job to compete with it."

That's what I'm worried about, too. The last thing I want to admit is that my drawer of sex toys might not be able to satisfy the needs I'll have after our night together, but I hope like hell I'll get over it.

I have to. There's no other choice.

Halfway to the greenhouse, Kiran does one of those one-handed turns of the steering wheel, and I swear the action speaks directly to my vagina, because I can literally feel my heartbeat down there.

Leaning my head back against the headrest, I close my eyes and slowly breathe in and out, trying to calm my body down.

"Thea," Kiran croaks. "I can smell you."

I peer over at him. "Excuse me? I showered."

He reaches a hand over the center console, placing it on my thigh and squeezing. "Your arousal. I can smell it. You're horny. What did it for you, baby?"

"You'll laugh at me."

His hand moves a little higher, bunching my skirt up, and his pinky dips down between my thighs, rubbing along my slit through my underwear. "Never. I like that something I do turns you on so much. Tell me so I can make sure to do it again."

Spreading my legs, I pull my skirt up even further, allowing him more access. What's one more orgasm for the road? A great way to start my morning before work, that's what.

"It's the way you turn the wheel with one hand in place. Fuck, it does something to me."

Kiran sneaks his hand in through the side of my underwear, immediately locating my clit and rubbing in circles so hard and dedicated that I'm already on the verge of letting go.

His truck slows before he turns again. "Like this, baby?" He inches through the turn, showcasing his expertise, and I come unglued.

"Yes! Oh, Kiran. Shit." The words tumble from my mouth one after the other as I ride the wave of ecstasy.

We bounce over a bump, and I squeal as his fingers move inside me, where he curls them before pulling his hand back out and inserting his fingers into his mouth. "Mmmm," he moans. "Delectable."

I smack his arm. "Would you stop?"

He shakes his head. "I will not. Your taste is unlike anything you can imagine. I'm thrilled to score another chance to get you off and taste you again."

I roll my head to look at him as I readjust my clothes. "What about you?"

Taking my chin between his thumb and forefinger, he gives it a playful squeeze. "I'll be okay, sweet girl. That was all about you."

"Thank you," I whisper. "You're a very sweet man, Kiran."

"And you're even sweeter," he murmurs back to me as we pull into the parking lot of his greenhouse, where a wave of sadness crashes over me.

I wish I could say I had the time, energy, and desire to explore things with Kiran, but I can't. I shouldn't. There are too many risks involved. Besides shifting part of my focus onto a partner and trying to fit them into my well-oiled schedule, there's the risk of getting hurt, yanking me ten steps backward.

Even though my last breakup was *my* choice, it still did something to me—something that has me wondering if a relationship is worth the worry. I'm comfortable with my life. Why risk it? Dating today sucks anyways—I've heard the stories.

Leaning over, he places a kiss on my temple. "Don't be a stranger, Thea. And thank you for a wonderful night."

I turn my head and crash my lips to his as if it'll be the last time, which I guess it is.

"My pleasure... Quite literally." I wink before grabbing my bag and getting out to head to my car.

"Thea!" Kiran calls after me.

I briskly walk back to his truck and open the door. "Yeah?"

"About my, uh, alien form. Can we agree to keep that between us?"

I nod. "Yeah, of course."

His eyes grow serious. "Not even your friend, Wren. Okay?"

"Got it, Kiran!" I shoot him a thumbs-up as I shut the door and head back toward my car.

As I back away from the greenhouse, Kiran—who's now standing out front—turns and waves at me.

He's dressed in khakis again, with an emerald-green hoodie that matches his eyes. His hair is a tousled mess from our evening of bliss, and his smile is warm and sweet as I wave back.

I can't help but wonder what it'd be like to come home to someone like him...

But I also wonder why talking about his alien form needs to be a secret...

CHAPTER THIRTEEN

KIRAN

It's been a week since my night with Thea, since I saw her last.

Seven whole days since my mouth was on her, since hers was on me, since I was inside her.

I've been forced to use my hand every night since, but it doesn't compare to her touch, her mouth, or her pussy.

Her body was made for me, and mine for her. I just need to make a plan that will help her see that it's okay to take a chance with me.

"You okay, boss?" Colton comes up beside me and asks.

He's a local community college student with hopes of studying botany and has been working here since he was able to get a job in high school. Great kid. Fantastic worker.

Only issue? He's a total meddler.

Moving the hose over to the next batch of plants, I sneak a peek at him. "Of course, why?"

He does a little tilt back and forth from his heels to the balls of his feet before settling back in place. "Well... It's just that... You were overwatering those orchids before I came up."

Sure as shit, there is an absolute pool of water beneath the stands of orchids.

"Damn it! Here!" I thrust the hose into Colton's hands. "Finish up while I save these things."

Colton doesn't even question me as he gets to work finishing up with the rest of the indoor plants. Meanwhile, I swear and complain under my breath the entire time I scurry to soak up the water. I have to remove my socks and shoes in order to absorb the massive puddle on the floor through my feet. Simultaneously, I forcefully sprout tiny roots from my fingers that extend to reach into each pot, where they then siphon the excess moisture from every orchid's soil.

By the time I finish rescuing the flowers, I slosh my way over to the alien section, desperate to empty my waterlogged body's reservoir into this section of plants in order to find some much-needed relief. Not a single droplet of water goes to waste in my greenhouse. Not if I can help it.

Then I hide away in my office for a break to clear my head.

"Wanna talk about it?" Colton takes me by surprise with his presence once again.

I can't help but roll my eyes before staring up at him as he leans against the doorframe. "About?"

His smirk leaks sarcasm. "The woman you're head over heels for."

"I'm not head over heels for *any* woman," I respond.

He crosses his arms. "*Yes*, you are."

"Am not."

"Are too."

"This is ridiculous." Using both hands, I attempt to stroke away the sudden headache pulsing in my temples. "I'm arguing like an adolescent *with* an adolescent."

He scoffs. "Aren't I technically a young adult now?"

Throwing up my hands in frustration, I move around to the front of my desk and perch on the edge. "Technicalities. Now, what do you want, Colton?"

An alien-like fire must cross my eyes, because Colton's gaze widens before settling again. "I want to know who—or what—has you so distracted. Maybe I can help."

"How the hell do you think a twenty-year-old such as yourself is going to help a man in his mid-thirties?"

He shrugs. "Well, I have a girlfriend. I'd like to think I understand ladies up to a point."

My left eye twitches as I mull over what to do and say with a long, deep sigh that escapes through my mouth. "You can't say a word."

I can't believe I'm actually considering this.

His thumb and forefingers touch before he zips them across his lips like a zipper.

"Her name's Thea," I start. "She came in here, busted a plant, caught my eye, and now I can't get her out of my mind."

Colton nods along with my words. "It was your precious penis plant, right?"

"My what?"

"You know. The only one of its kind. Looks like a penis. You checked on it at *least* once a day. That one."

I can't contain my raised brows. "I didn't realize I made it that apparent..."

"Did you sleep with her after she bought your penis plant, concurrently stealing your heart?"

"We shouldn't be talking about this." I shake my head. I knew this was a bad idea. "It's inappropriate."

He laughs. "To talk about sex with a fellow adult?"

Walking closer, I lower my voice. "You're *barely* one."

A smile pulls up at the corner of his mouth. "So you *did* sleep with her. How was it?"

Tongue in my cheek, I head straight back to my desk. I shouldn't say anything. Right?

"Me and my girl," he starts. "We—"

"Nope!" I hold up a hand. "No. I don't wanna know. It was great, okay? Best night of my life, and now I can't stop thinking about her. There. Happy now?"

Colton nods as a humongous grin grows on his face. "Very. Now, let's make a plan for you to see her again."

CHAPTER FOURTEEN

THEA

"You mean to tell me that you had the best sex of your life, *all night long*, mind you, and you haven't gone back for more?" Wren questions from across the table, nearly spilling her beer in her shock and dismay. "What the fuck is wrong with you? It's a Valentine's miracle!"

I purse my lips as I angrily fork at my salad starter. We're doing our weekly girl dinner at a local bar and grill, and I'm giving her the best lowdown I can on my wild sexcapade night without bringing up the other form of Kiran that fucked me silly.

"Wren, please." I think about my words carefully while I chew a bite of lettuce before gulping it down. "You know what my schedule is like. I make overtime look like child's play, and I'm exhausted when I'm not at work. I don't know how many times I have to say this."

She slams a hand on the table. "But yet, you're at dinner with me."

"You're incorrigible."

"No. I'm right." Wren reaches over to take one of my hands in hers. "Love is fucking scary, Thea. Everyone is working their asses off. Life is busy for all of us. I think everyone struggles with mental health in some fashion. The entire damn world is beyond exhausted. We could all make up excuse after excuse for the rest of our days. But we won't find the one we're destined for by always running away from taking the leap. There's someone out there for all of us who will understand our schedules, our mental state, and our lives. I think you should go for it. You told Kiran what's going on. You guys could make it work. You rock at being alone, but there's nothing wrong with being with someone either. Especially if it's what you want."

I gulp, pulling my hand away. "I don't know if I'm ready."

She laughs, her beautifully crooked smile brightening her entire face. "Are any of us?"

"I guess not... I just—I don't know, Wren. I don't think it's a good idea."

"Well, you know what?"

I quirk a brow at her question.

"I'm rooting for Kiran, and that's all I'm going to say."

Yeah... Maybe I'm secretly rooting for Kiran, too.

By the time I get home from the restaurant, it takes everything in me to shower, change into my pajamas, and carry Willy to the kitchen for some TLC. I'd like to prune his leaves, wipe down the outside of his pot, and get him watered.

I think I'm really starting to love this guy. Is it normal to *love* a plant? Maybe it's because I named him and even wrote it in permanent marker on his pot?

Getting him to the kitchen counter, I can't help but cradle his penile arm in my hand. Why, I don't know. Okay. Maybe I do. Maybe—*just* maybe—I'm missing Kiran and his phenomenal dick.

But I'm keeping that secret to myself.

DING DONG.

"Damn it!" I yell, accidentally cracking off Willy's willy in the process of getting startled. "Not again. Oh, Willy. I'm so sorry. Just one second. I bet your Aunt Wren is here to bother me some more."

With angry feet, I trudge to the door and peek through the peephole to find—

Wait a second.

"Kiran?" I whisper.

What the hell is he doing here?

Carefully unlocking and opening the door, I come face-to-face with the alien god himself, unable to contain the smile that overtakes my face at the full-toothed grin he's donning.

"What are you doing here? At ten o'clock at night?" I question. "And how did you even figure out where I live?"

Kiran's eyes widen as they flick between my face and my...body? Is he checking me out in my pajamas? They're just a ratty pair of sleep shorts and a tank. Nothing to write home about, surely.

"Should I be worried?" he asks.

My face contorts of its own accord. "What? Why?"

He points at my—oh, shit—the damn plant penis that is broken and in my hand!

"Ohhhhh, that. Well—you see... Long story short, the doorbell startled me as I was taking care of Willy, and his willy sort of...snapped off—again..." I cringe at the admission. "Poor thing is rather delicate."

Kiran laughs. "You were taking care of Willy? In what way? Should I be jealous?"

Leaning out of the doorway, I thwack him on the chest. "No, you pervert. Get your head out of the gutter."

He raises his hands in mock surrender. "No can do, sweet girl. I'm around you, remember? Which means my mind is already there."

I roll my eyes. "What do you want, Kiran?"

The paper bag sitting in the crook of his elbow crinkles as he lowers his forearms. "How do you feel about dessert?"

"Uh, good? Who doesn't like dessert?"

He shrugs. "Serial killers?"

My head flies back with uncontrollable laughter. "Do you want to come in before I wake up the neighbors? We can talk more about dessert and serial killers when you're out of the cold."

Hopefully, he can save my plant's penis while he's here.

CHAPTER FIFTEEN

KIRAN

Thea's house is very cozy and tidy. Wood floors cover every room I can see from the entryway, which includes the kitchen, dining room, and living room. Even the hallway opening up ahead and to the right has wood.

It's weird that I'm focusing so much on the floors, but being a big plant guy, I think about the trees that went into creating such gorgeous planks. They make for easy cleanup and all that, but were more trees planted to replace the ones cut down? I certainly hope so.

"Kiran?" Thea calls.

I turn my attention from the wood planks to her in the kitchen.

She's perfect. Comfy in her pajamas, hair up in a bun, and...*sockless*?

"Aren't your feet cold?" I wonder aloud.

Thea gives me a bewildered look before gazing down and between both of our feet. "A little? I hate wearing socks to bed. I can't breathe in them. You came just as I was preparing to go to sleep."

I cringe. "I'm sorry. I—I know it's late, but…" Should I be honest? I should. Colton told me to be honest.

"But what?"

"I wanted to see you." My admission flies out quickly.

She turns to face me, dropping the penis at the same time. "Oh, shit." Thea reaches down for the plant piece. "Sorry about that, but, um, what did you say?"

Judging by the way her hands can't seem to get a firm grasp on Willy, I'd say she's a bit nervous, for Pete's sake. Speaking of which, who is Pete? Oh my word. Now I'm talking to myself.

There seems to be a hint of humor hiding in that minuscule uptick in the left corner of her mouth she's fighting.

"You want me to repeat myself?"

She nods.

"Okay, sweet girl. Fine." I take a step closer, noticing how her breathing picks up. "I wanted to see you because, for the last week, you're all I've thought about."

I'm even closer now, mere inches from being able to touch her. "So much so that I've been fucking up at work and had to ask a twenty-year-old how I could go about seeing you again."

A wheeze filters through the air, and my eyes scan the room for any signs of trouble until I notice that the noise is coming from Thea. And I only know that because of the way her body is shaking and her hand is attempting to hide a smile.

"What's so funny?" I ask, embarrassment beginning to creep in.

She lowers her hand. "Why a twenty-year-old?"

I shrug. "He's the one who told me I was fucking up at work. He wanted to know what woman was taking up residence in my mind, and he wanted to help me out. I don't know. Colton was just there, and I sort of word-vomited."

Thea slowly blinks as she sets down the castrated plant and closes the distance between us before placing a hand on my chest. "Colton, huh?"

My head bobs up and down as I inhale a big gulp of air. Having her this close to me again is setting my body on fire, and the heat starts where she's touching me.

"Seems like a good seed," she says, her voice taking on a flirtatious tone at the same time the scent of her arousal hits my nose.

"Thea," I croak, leaning my head down closer.

She reaches up on her tiptoes to kiss the side of my jaw. "I wanted to see you, too, Kiran. Think you'll fit in my bed?"

As if my dick wasn't already standing at attention.

I've slept with human women before, not many, but I have. Not a single one of those times ever felt like my one night with Thea.

Granted, I obviously hadn't transformed because they weren't my mates, but that's beside the point.

Thea is the only one I want, and I'm going to pull out every page in the book to try to win her over. To make her mine.

"Lead the way, baby." I swoop her up, and she squeals in surprise. "Use your finger, Thea. Point out where to go."

She points toward the hallway. I begin walking that way, nipping at a finger of the hand she's resting on my shoulder at the same time.

Her room is the last one on the right. Three of the walls are cream-colored, while the fourth is a very light periwinkle that matches her bedspread.

Before I can make any more assessments, I let Thea slide down my body. And once she reaches the floor, she takes my hand in hers and leads me to the bed. My transformation has already begun. I can tell by how tight my jeans are getting around my thighs.

"How do you feel about sixty-nine, Kiran?" Thea asks, stopping us next to her bed, where she begins working on my pants.

I quirk a brow at her. "Sixty-nine?"

Her eyes widen. "You've never heard of sixty-nine? Have you slept with other human women?"

Guilt sweeps through me. Why do I suddenly wish I would've saved myself for her? For my mate?

But how was I supposed to know I'd ever find her? Not all of us do. "Kiran."

My eyes snap to hers.

"What is it?"

I grind my teeth. "I feel bad talking about it."

"Why?"

"Isn't it...rude?"

After pushing my pants down my legs, along with my boxer briefs, she ditches her clothes in record time, prompting me to remove my own shirt next, until we're both standing face-to-face and bare naked.

She offers me a sympathetic grin. "No, Kiran. I mean, if you're rubbing something in my face, then yeah. But no, I don't think there's anything wrong with talking about past experiences this way. I asked. I'm an open book. I can answer an intimate question you have, if it helps."

My stomach sours. I'm not sure I want to know anything about her past experiences—definitely not the shitty men that didn't make her happy. My discomfort must show on my face, because Thea chuckles to herself.

"Or not," she adds. "Why don't we just forget I asked? Lie down on the bed, and I'll gladly teach you some math."

CHAPTER SIXTEEN

THEA

Kiran is here.

In my house.

In my bed.

Maybe Wren was right. Maybe kismet and fate really do exist.

Maybe I'll find out, because after tonight, I think I'll be open to seeing what happens.

He came looking for me because he wanted to see me. Big, strong, alien Kiran. He came looking for me—a human—when I hadn't planned on seeing him again unless I went to that greenhouse. It's like a scene from a book.

And that right there is the reason he might stand a chance of convincing me of just about anything after tonight.

"What now?" Kiran asks. He's lying in the middle of my bed, staring up at the ceiling as his head rests on my pillow. His lower half has already transformed, raised tattoos and all.

I crawl up onto the bed and move between his legs. "Well, we definitely need to get the rest of you to change, don't you think? I'm desperate for some more of that tongue-root action."

His deep laughter sends the butterflies in my stomach soaring.

He lifts his head to peer down at me. "How do you plan on doing that, Thea?"

Oh, he knows exactly what he's doing. His voice is quite literally dripping in sex, and I love it.

"This," I reply, leaning down to take his member in my mouth.

The sudden action must somehow startle him subconsciously, because his legs jolt before they resettle on either side of me.

"Oh, Thea." He groans, grabbing onto the back of my head.

Bobbing up and down, I hollow out my cheeks each time I bring my head up, making him inhale sharply through his teeth as he attempts to keep his composure.

I throw in a little moan at the end, which has him fisting my hair and trying to make me move faster. But instead, I pull off with a *pop* and stare up at him through hooded eyes.

"How was that?"

He gives me a drowsy smirk as his deep emerald eyes glow with desire. "Amazing. Please don't say you're done."

The rest of his tattoos have finished forming along the sides of his face and down the rest of his body. The leaves and twigs have also sprouted throughout his now-tousled hair.

I caught him yanking on a handful of the strands at one point while I was down there blowing him, which pleases me more than anything.

I love the idea of being able to make a man come completely unglued with my touch alone. And the fact that my mouth was able to draw this sort of reaction out of him really excites me for what's to come.

"Not done, handsome. Sixty-nine is up next on the menu. I just need you to lie there while I get in position."

I crawl along the side of him toward the headboard, and he palms one of my breasts in his large hand the moment I'm close enough.

Then I swing a leg over his face, positioning myself over his mouth, and he releases a, "*Mmm*."

"I already like sixty-nine." Looping his arms around my hips, he clasps my ass in both of his hands and places a chaste kiss to my core.

"Mmm," I moan. "Just wait until you see what we do now."

Walking my hands down his torso that's covered in stretches of such soft, sage skin between sinewy patches of bark, I position my head over his dick, tracing a few of his vine-like tattoos along his hip bones with one of my fingers.

His cock bobs up and down before I take it in my hand and kiss the tip.

Kiran growls. He actually growls, and the sound is like some secret language that only my vagina understands. "What are we fucking doing, Thea? Because your beautiful, glistening pussy is in my face, and I'd love nothing more than to make you scream my name."

My eyes roll back in my head a little at his dirty words. "Next is the best part, Kiran. Now that we're in position, we both get to work on each other."

"So, you're going to suck my dick while I eat your pussy?"

"Mhm," I answer, licking my lips in anticipation.

He pushes down on my lower back, forcing my hips to open wider. "Then, by all means, suffocate the fuck out of me, sweet girl. I want you to be all I see, smell, taste, and feel."

I'm about to ask about the last sense when he interrupts me. "And as for hearing, my name better be one of the words you scream with my hard cock in your mouth."

Holy fucking shit...

CHAPTER SEVENTEEN

KIRAN

Between Thea's mouth licking and sucking my cock, her wandering hands, and the delicious work I'm putting in on her, I'm learning that sixty-nine has a lot of things to focus on.

It's pleasing to hear just how much she likes this too. Every time I even lick or nip at her bud, she moans around my shaft, inching me closer and closer to release.

Pushing a finger inside her wet heat, I place the tip of my tongue directly on her clit, already anticipating the noises I'll earn from my girl as the roots work in tandem with my licks.

One vibrating lick is all it takes to have her bucking against my face and moaning, the reverberations dancing along my dick.

"Yeah? You like that, baby?"

She answers with a short moan—it almost sounds...frustrated—and nudges my lips with her pussy, begging me for more stimulation.

And that's exactly what I give her.

I push a second finger into her core, thrusting in and out at a steady pace as my other hand travels down her body, where I pinch one of her nipples between two of my fingers.

Then I lick and suck at her swollen clit like a man lost in a desert who's just found his only source of water to survive off of.

All of this has Thea picking up speed as she works her mouth and tongue on and around my cock, toying with my balls in one of her hands.

We're both close. I know she can feel my balls drawing up closer and closer to my body, and I can feel the way her muscles are squeezing tighter and tighter around my fingers like a vise.

I pull my mouth away from her core for just a second. "Thea, baby. I need you to come all over me, okay?"

"Yes, Kiran. Fuck, yes. At the same time."

Our mouths are back on each other.

I'm thrusting into her mouth as she rides my face.

Moans and muffled words bounce off every surface of the room until...

Both of us come undone at the same time.

My seed spurts into her mouth, and her tongue rubs against my shaft as she swallows it down with precision.

Meanwhile, I lap up her juices as they slowly slide down my fingers and between her lips.

"So good, sweet girl. You taste so fucking good," I praise her.

Thea carefully releases me, her breathing heavy and labored. "Kiran, I don't know what to say."

I give her ass a playful slap. "What do you mean?"

"That was the best face-fucking of my entire life."

"Well, Thea." I give her pussy one last peck. "I'd gladly do that every day of the week if you asked me to."

She laughs as she maneuvers herself from above me to beside me, lying on my chest as I wrap an arm around her.

Cuddling is one of my favorite things, and the fact that I'm getting to cuddle my mate? Pure perfection.

If only she knew what she was to me.

If only I knew she wanted me the same way that I want her.

Maybe I'll get the chance to tell her someday...

I just hope it doesn't scare her away.

As my body changed back into its human form, Thea slept for thirty minutes while snuggled close to me. The restful sound of her quiet breathing nearly lulled me to sleep as well, but I didn't want to miss any time with her, especially if this might be it.

Who am I to assume that something will come of it just because she let me in tonight? No one. Assuming is a one-way ticket to heartbreak.

"Kiran?" her delicate voice whispers.

I continue my gentle strokes up and down her arm. "Yes, sweet girl?"

She tilts her face up to look at mine. "I broke Willy again."

Laughter spills out of me, her head bouncing up and down with the shaking of my chest. "Yeah, I saw that. Thought maybe you were taking out some anger on me through Willy or something."

"No." She bats at my pec. "But do you think you can fix him? Ya know...again?"

I flatten out my arm so Thea can roll out of bed and follow after her. She pulls on my T-shirt that reaches past her bottom, and I yank on my underwear and jeans.

In the kitchen, I get to work on healing the plant, my fingers glowing with highlighter-yellow power.

While the power works its magic, Thea peers into the paper bag I brought.

"Shit," I half-yell, startling her from her inquisition. "That needed to go in the freezer!"

"Look away," she orders, crinkling the bag and holding it behind her back.

I do, listening intently for her next move, which involves the thud of a trash can lid and footsteps back to my side.

She kisses my shoulder before opening the freezer, the chilly air reaching up and through the fibers of my jeans. "Do you like ice cream?"

My eyes drift right to hers. "Yes, that's why—"

"Good thing you came tonight." She cuts me off. "My grocery pickup is for tomorrow, and I need to get rid of this pint. I'll grab two spoons and meet you on the couch, okay?"

Warm, hopeful feelings swim in my chest as she leaves the room, taking my heart with her. I could get used to this. I could get used to her.

To *us*.

CHAPTER EIGHTEEN

THEA

Once Kiran enters the living room, he relaxes himself into the chaise. His legs dangle over the edge a bit, due to his height, and he waves me over to sit between them.

I hand him a spoon and lay a blanket over his lap before cuddling in, taking another spoonful of the Neapolitan ice cream once I'm settled.

"Why did you only put the blanket over me?" he asks.

I hold up the pint so he can take a spoonful next. "Because I have no underwear on, and I didn't want to put my bare ass on the couch."

He laughs against me, and I can't help but close my eyes and smile at how good it feels.

Kiran is so warm, funny, sweet, and authentic. Whatever it is about him, I have felt safe from the very moment I laid eyes on him, even when he was basically chewing me out for injuring a precious plant.

Taking another large spoonful, he moans a little as he puts it in his mouth. "A Neapolitan girl, huh? I feel like that's a very uncommon flavor."

"I agree." I nod. "And I don't understand why. I mean, the three main flavors of ice cream, all put into one? How can you possibly go wrong?"

"You can't," he agrees. "This was a good choice. Better than what I brought."

I lean to face him. "What did you bring?"

He grimaces. "Butter pecan and mint chocolate chip."

"Ew, Kiran! Those are senior citizen flavors."

We finish off the pint fairly quickly, thanks to Kiran's large scoops. He takes the empty container from me, putting the lid back on and setting it and our licked-clean spoons on the table that runs along the back of the couch before grabbing both of my hands in one of his and holding them above our heads.

I can't help but squeal. "Kiran!"

"What did you call my ice cream flavors?"

My attempts to break free are futile. Not that I'm trying all that hard, because I'm definitely getting turned on, yet again.

"Senior citizen flavors."

His free hand cups one of my breasts, and he pinches at my nipple through the fabric of his shirt I'm wearing. Then his mouth is against my ear. "That's not very nice, Thea. What do you think naughty girls like yourself should get for being so mean?"

Oh. I think I'm going to like this game. "An orgasm?"

He licks up the column of my neck before nipping at my earlobe. "You do, huh? I'd have to agree, but you're going to have to show me."

Now I really do try to break free, because I have no clue what that means, but my strength is nothing compared to his.

Kiran kisses along my jaw before putting his mouth to my ear again. "I'm going to take this shirt off of you, Thea. Then I'm going to free your hands so you can bring *yourself* to orgasm."

"Wait, what?"

"You heard me." He pulls the shirt over my head before releasing my hands to take it the rest of the way off. "I want to watch you touch yourself, sweet girl."

That's not what I was expecting him to say. "Um... I—"

I attempt to argue, but the way Kiran is sucking on my neck, cupping both of my breasts, and playing with my nipples makes me lose my train of thought.

"What was that, baby?"

A moan breaks free as I lean my head back into his chest. "Kiran, uh. I want *you* to touch me." My words come out between choppy breaths. "Please."

Freeing one of my breasts, he brings that hand to the back of my neck, moves my hair over my shoulder, and kisses just beneath my hairline as he breathes in deep. "And I want to watch you touch yourself. For me. *Please?*"

Kiran takes one of my hands in his as the other continues kneading my chest and trails our hands down my stomach, over my mound, and between my legs. Leaving my hand there, Kiran spreads my legs further apart and then places his hand back over mine.

He takes my middle finger and presses it directly to my clit. "Thea, I know for a fact you touch yourself. So, show me what you do when no one is around. Let me see how you make yourself come undone."

Slowly, I swirl my finger over my swollen bud, but my self-consciousness sinks in. "I don't know, Kiran. I feel weird about this."

"Why?"

"I'm kinda embarrassed? I don't know..."

Kiran kisses the back of my head. "Don't be, baby. I promise you, I've wanted to watch this since the moment I laid eyes on you. There's nothing to be embarrassed about. You're gorgeously sexy, and you're safe with me."

Within two seconds, I throw caution to the wind, settle into Kiran's body, and close my eyes. Just like I always do, I dip my middle finger down to gather some of my wetness that I then drag up to my clit before rubbing in small circles again.

It doesn't take long to work myself up to making sounds, because there's something about knowing Kiran is watching me pleasure myself that riles me up.

"Fuck," I whisper, the pressure inside my body rising. "Mmm. Yes."

Kiran groans above me, his cock growing harder and harder with each passing minute. "Fuck, Thea. Keep going."

I do.

Adding a second finger, I swirl around and around my clit as Kiran palms my breasts again, his hips slightly bucking up against my back to gain some friction.

"I'm getting close," I tell him. "Uh, Kiran. I'm almost there."

"Yes, sweet girl. Fuck yes. Come for me, baby. *Now*."

The pressure swirls in my belly, and then my body twitches and convulses as the waves of my orgasm crash through me over and over again. All the while, Kiran holds me to him, kissing and nipping at my ear and neck as my body begins to relax into post-orgasmic bliss.

"Thea," he murmurs.

I lick my lips as my eyes remain closed. "Hmm?"

"That was the hottest thing I've watched in my entire life."

I chuckle. "You've never watched porn, Kiran?"

"Porn could never compare, baby. No way in hell."

After using the blanket to wipe myself off, I fold it in half, turn to face Kiran, and sit down...naked. "You know what this means, big guy?"

He tilts his head in question.

"Your turn."

CHAPTER NINETEEN

KIRAN

"I think I'd rather just fuck you to another orgasm," I reply. "Come here."

She shakes her head at me, her eyes sweeping me up and down in my now-transformed body. "Show me, Kiran. Show me how you play with your cock when no one's around."

The way her tongue swipes out to lick along the seam of her mouth, the tip slightly cupping her top lip, has me heaving a heavy breath.

I lock my eyes on hers as I unbutton and unzip my pants, lifting my hips up just a little to shimmy my jeans down until my cock springs free.

It's hard, throbbing, and standing at attention, putting on a show as Thea stares down at it as if it's her next meal.

Grasping my dick in my hand, I swirl the pad of my thumb around the tip of my head, rolling the drop of precum around the crown before I apply pressure and give my penis one long, slow pump to the base of my shaft.

My balls are already beginning to pull up toward my body because of the way Thea watches me.

Moving closer, she pulls my pants and underwear the rest of the way off before lying on her stomach between my legs.

Her tits are bolstered up with the pressure of the cushion, which has my mouth dropping open.

"Damn, Thea. Your tits. Mmm."

"You like them being so close to your hard cock, Kiran?" She lowers her mouth to the top of my thighs, peppering kisses on one and then the other. "Stroke yourself, baby. I want you to come on me."

Hearing those words fall from her lips is all it takes for me to pick up the pace. It never takes me long to work myself over, and now that the woman plastered in all my recent fantasies is perched up in between my legs, I know it will take even less time than normal.

"Spit on it, sweet girl."

She crawls closer, hanging her head over the tip of my cock and slowly letting some saliva drip onto it. The wetness slides down, over, and in between my fingers, and I have to lay my head back against the couch and close my eyes for a second to gather myself. And while I do, I work her spit over me, pumping up and down with renewed ease now that I have some lubrication.

I snap my head back up and lock eyes with her, showing her exactly how I like to pleasure myself when I'm alone. Stroking from base to tip, I pump faster and faster, moans and groans spilling from my mouth.

"Uhhh, fuck. Yes. Damn it. Thea, turn over for me, sweet girl. Uh, I need to come on those perfect tits, baby. Hurry."

Thea quickly turns over, pushing her tits together with her hands as I lean up and over her, planting my free hand beside her hip. She leans her head up to kiss my balls, and I come so hard, I see stars.

My cum spurts onto her chest, dripping down her cleavage, and if I could come a second time this soon, I fucking would. Especially when Thea begins rubbing my release all over her breasts, smoothing it over her skin like a lotion.

One of her fingers scoops some up and smears it on her tongue while I watch. She closes her mouth around it and sucks it off with a pop.

"I think you should sit back down, Kiran."

Still peering down at her, I arch a brow. "Because?"

She shoots me a sinful smirk. "Because I'd like to go for a ride."

Thirty minutes and another orgasm for each of us later, Thea and I have cleaned up, showered, and crawled our way back into her bed.

Her long hair is silky and damp as I run my fingers through it.

"Thea, would you like to go on a date with me?"

She titters. "A bit late for a date, don't ya think?"

Even though she's not looking at me, I roll my eyes. "It's never too late for one. We're allowed to be a little unconventional."

"Okay," she agrees, smiling against my chest. "This coming weekend. A date. Me and you."

"I have to wait the whole week?"

She cuddles closer, her body molding against mine, beginning to melt into me as exhaustion sets in. "Well, yeah. I'm a busy woman. I've gotta make it through the week first."

That's what I like about Thea. She is a strong, independent, hard-working woman. It seems to me that she's been doing life alone for a long time, and while I'd never snuff out that spark, I hope that someday I can convince her it's okay to receive help.

Strong, hyper-independent people deserve love, too—if they want it.

And damn it, I hope she wants it.

CHAPTER TWENTY

THEA

While I was excited for the weekend itself, my date with Kiran to-morrow was what really pulled me through yet another hectic work week. Wren insisted on coming over here for our girls' night because I worked late every single day, per usual.

I'm so lucky to have Wren for a best friend. She's a cosmetologist, and she works really hard to give herself a great work-life balance. I wish I had that and could follow her advice to not give so much of myself to my job that it consumes everything.

But the fact of the matter is, even in my thirties, I still have no idea what the fuck I want to do with my life. So until I figure it out, I'll run myself into the ground, hoping like hell I can build a life for myself where I someday have the freedom to maybe do something I've always wanted to do.

Like opening up a restaurant where everything is served flight style. Burger flights, taco flights, appetizer flights. In honor of all those—like me—who are creatures of habit when ordering out but still want to try something new; having a sampler-type plate of options meets both of those requests.

For now, it'll stay a dream...

"Soooooo, what are you guys going to do on your date?" Wren asks, staring at my reflection in the mirror as she curls my hair so it's ready for tomorrow.

I shrug. "No idea. He just told me to meet him at his greenhouse."

She wiggles her brows. "Do you think he's going to fuck you silly in an open bag of soil or something?"

"Soil?" My face crinkles before a guffaw spurts out of me. "What about that would be even slightly enjoyable?"

Her jaw slides back and forth. "The fact that you guys would get dirty while *getting dirty*?"

I shake my head, accidentally pulling on my hair that's still wrapped around the curler. "You're ridiculous."

"You love me anyway."

"Always will," I reply.

Finishing my style with a few spritzes of hairspray, she gives my hair a quick zhuzh and grabs onto my shoulders. "Promise me that if Kiran has any hot, alien friends, you'll send them my way. Whatever sex you're getting served seems better than anything any human man could possibly offer."

"What makes you say that?" I question.

She smiles sweetly at me. "Because you are positively glowing, and no matter what you say, you seem open to taking a chance on him. And that right there is why I'm still rooting for him."

It's dark out, the greenhouse parking lot is empty, and the glow from inside the building is soft and flickering. I focus on the way the gravel crunches beneath my sneakers as I make my way up to the entrance, daydreaming about what this date might bring.

Kiran told me to dress casually for what he has planned tonight. *A night of comfort and cum* is what he jokingly texted. And while I may have sent an eye roll emoji, I secretly am hoping he plans to keep his word about those two things.

Pushing open the door, I peek my head in. "Kiran?" I call out.

"Hi there." The voice comes from a young man who just popped up from behind the cashier counter.

"Hi," I answer. "Is Kiran here?"

He smiles warmly at me. "Oh, yes. He's just about ready. My name is Colton." He wipes his hand off on his apron before offering it to me. "I've heard a lot about you."

Shock swims through me before realization sets in. So this is the twenty-year-old advice-giver. "You have, huh?"

"Well, yeah." He chortles. "Who do you think convinced him to show up at your house with ice cream? That man doesn't even know how to search the internet for people very well. I was able to find your address in under five minutes."

My eyes widen. "That's rather...terrifying."

He shrugs. "The internet has its pros and cons. But anyway, I'm going to head out so I can lock you guys in. Enjoy your date." Colton shoots me a wink.

As he makes his way to the door, I feel like I owe him my gratitude for what he's done. If Kiran hadn't shown up at my house, I probably wouldn't be here right now, taking a chance on what could possibly be fate.

"Thank you, Colton."

All he does is give me a nod before slipping out the door.

"Thea?" Kiran calls out as soon as the door locks. "Are you here?"

I follow his voice, a flickering glow from a room down a hallway guiding the way. And when I reach the first and only doorway with actual light emanating from within, I enter and gasp.

Lit candles line the floor along each wall, and in the middle of the room is a table with two pots, a small container of soil, and various plants, seedlings, and bulbs.

"What is this?" I ask, smiling wide at Kiran, who is standing beside the table, looking nervous, with his hands in his pockets.

Walking toward me, he takes my hands in his. "Well, when you first entered my shop, I overheard your displeasure at buying plants, only for them to die, so I thought we could actually plant some of your own, rather than giving you a bouquet you'd have to place in a vase."

I wrap my arms around his waist, prompting him to wrap himself around me.

"I don't know what to say, Kiran. This is very sweet of you."

Greenery might be growing on me—even outside of Willy—and I owe it all to Kiran. Okay, and maybe Willy, too.

CHAPTER TWENTY-ONE

KIRAN

Thea's hair smells like grapefruit, and I can't help but take a big whiff of her fruity scent as I hold her tight against me.

"Anything for you, sweet girl," I breathe against the top of her head. "Come on. Sit down."

Leading her to the table, I slide my chair over to sit on the same side as her and hand her the terracotta pot I prepped for her.

Strewn across the table are various types of succulents and other beginner plants, along with a mass of gardening tools. I wait for her to see the surprise I got for her.

Thea gasps. "Are those tiny tools in a bag? Are they for me?!" Her voice raises an octave with every word. "Oh my gosh, Kiran! I want to pinch them."

I laugh. "They are for you. I thought you'd like them. You can use them while we plant some succulents."

She nods. "And why are we planting succulents?"

"Well, they're one of the easiest plants for people to grow and take care of. With your plant aversion, I figured they'd be the easiest bet."

"You'd be correct in assuming that. But still...*apologize.*"

"For what?" I ask, a smile pulling up at the corner of my mouth.

She levels me with a piercing stare. "For assuming I'd need something as *easy to plant* as succulents. That's rude."

I smack a hand to my chest. "I'm sorry I offended you, but am I wrong?"

A loud groan falls from her lips as her eyes roll back so far in her head, I'm sure she looked at her brain. "Whatever, Kiran. What the fuck everrrrrrr."

About an hour later, we've planted, laughed, and cleaned up in the bathroom.

"Colton should be here any minute now," I announce while we wait by the entrance.

Thea looks over from the bouquet display wall. "And what is Colton coming for?"

I smile. "He's bringing us our dinner."

The second my answer is out of my mouth, there's a knock on the door. "It's me, boss."

When I open the door, Colton strides in with two bags that I take from his hands. "Let me put these in the back room. I'll be right back."

Colton was kind enough to go grab my pickup order from the nearest Japanese steakhouse. I ordered both chicken and steak hibachi, some sushi, rice, soups, and starter salads. Hopefully, among all of the choices, there will be something Thea will like. That's one reason I planned this date the way I did—to give myself a chance to learn some more things about her. It was fairly easy getting her to open up as we put together the succulents, and now, I can commit to memory what she prefers from the spread I had delivered.

Once I have the containers opened and ready to go, I snag some waters from my office refrigerator and head back to where Thea and Colton are chatting.

What I find nearly stops me in my tracks.

Thea seems stiff, her hands gripping each other tightly as she peers at Colton with a questioning gaze.

"Well, I better head out, Kiran. I'll see you on Monday." He runs out the door like the building's on fire, while Thea continues staring after him, even after he has disappeared.

I take a few steps toward her, unsure of what happened. "Are you okay?"

"I'm not sure..." Her voice is quiet, and her eyes remain trained on the door, as if she might flee.

Moving even closer, I stand in her field of vision. "Did Colton say something to you?"

I can't imagine Colton would ever say something to offend someone, but nothing else happened, at least, not that I know of.

"Something about how I purchased a love plant that you've protected since you placed it in the greenhouse when I came here with Wren. What did he mean by that, Kiran?"

Shit...

CHAPTER TWENTY-TWO

THEA

Kiran stares at me with wide eyes, silently confirming my suspicion that Colton accidentally revealed something either he shouldn't have or that Kiran wasn't ready to tell me yet.

He hooked ya with that love plant, didn't he?

That's what Colton had said—or joked—and that's what keeps playing in my mind. The only plant I've purchased from here, besides Wren's bouquet items, was…Willy. And what does it mean for Willy to be a love plant?

The fact that Kiran is an alien leaves every single possibility to chance. How am I supposed to know what all these alien plants do? For all I know, there could be medicinal cures in this greenhouse just waiting to be discovered.

"I can explain," Kiran starts. "Let's go talk about it over dinner, okay? Please, Thea."

I shake my head. "I want to know right now. Is Willy some sort of love plant? And what the fuck does that even mean?"

Kiran runs a hand through his hair. "It's complicated..."

"Did you make me fall in love with you through that fucking plant, Kiran?" Fury rages through me like an angry bull, burning me from the inside out. It's too hot in here. My hands are sweaty, and my heart is racing.

"Plants from my planet can do all sorts of things, but there's no plant to make someone fall in love. That would be some sort of magic-type shit. A Talahecksiya is—"

I close the distance between us, staring up into his beautiful face, feeling beyond betrayed. "Spit it out, Kiran. Right fucking now," I seethe.

He licks his lips before puffing out a short breath of air. "As an alien species, we are known as the Dyv'i. However, there are dozens of subspecies that came over from Dyv'iëdus. I'm obviously one of the ones directly connected to plant life, known as the Cēd'oh. Aliens are destined to find a mate in life, all in their own way." He pauses far too long before adding what I've been dreading to hear. "I've had that Talahecksiya since I was an adolescent. I brought it to Earth with me and stationed it in the midst of that display." His finger points in the direction of the alien section. "And ever since, I've anxiously awaited the day it would attract my mate."

"I'm sorry..." My eyes can't stop blinking of their own accord, as if they're in just as much disbelief as I am. "Attract your *mate*? What exactly does that mean?"

Kiran fixes his gaze on the floor. "It emits an undetectable, yet specialized scent that can only attract our fated mate. To everyone else, the invisible scent repels them, keeping it on the shelf until the *one* discovers it."

"*The one*?" I screech. "Are you saying that I was drawn to Willy because of his scent? And that it inherently means that I'm *supposedly* the one destined for you?" I'm sure to add air quotes to go along with my tone. Kiran needs to know that I am far from happy about this.

He continues to avoid my eyes.

"Did you love potion me?" I wonder aloud. "Would I have ever been interested in you if it hadn't been for that stupid plant?"

He deflates in front of me, pain lacing every single one of his features. I probably took that last question a bit too far, but I'm angry. He should've told me. This all seems so wrong.

Grabbing my coat from the hook behind the cashier station, I hurriedly push my arms through it, feeling for my keys so I can make a mad dash out of here. I need to get away from him before he clouds my senses.

Kiran stations himself against the front door. "Please, don't leave like this, Thea. Let me explain more."

Exasperatedly, I march toward him as I throw my hands in the air. "What is left to explain, Kiran? You set up a decoy to find your mate, and the scent worked on me. I wasn't even looking for anyone! You lured me in like prey!" I'm jabbing his chest with my finger now. "I was doing just fucking fine on my own! Busy with work, exhausted from work. Work, work, work, work, work. I don't need anyone, and I definitely don't need you!"

The end of my rant has Kiran moving aside to grant me access to the door. "It wasn't a trick, Thea. It was fate. That's how the plant works. Come talk to me about this, ask me all the questions you want. None of this is a trick. It's destiny."

His eyes flash that emerald green I'm used to only seeing in the bedroom now. It draws up another question in me.

"You've slept with other humans before, right?"

He nods.

"And do you morph into your alien form for all of us?"

This time, he hesitates and then shakes his head.

I close my eyes, my forehead scrunching.

"Our mates are the only ones who will ever see us in our true form, and it's always when we're most intimate."

No wonder he asked me to keep our experience a secret. He knew it'd reveal the truth before he could gather the courage to do it.

Ripping open the door, I point my finger from me to him. "We are nothing, Kiran. *You* tricked me. Fuck destiny."

I slam the door, stomping to my car in the cold, dark night.

CHAPTER TWENTY-THREE

KIRAN

I'm fairly certain the booming echoes of the door slamming in my mind are going to drive me crazy... Maybe I'm already there.

I can't resist pacing back and forth from the front door to the alien section I set up that caused all of this. And all the while, I alternate between checking my phone and peeking out the door to see if Thea has returned.

Please let all of this just be some terrible nightmare.

Then I do the only thing I can think of. I call Colton. The twenty-year-old community college student has no business meddling in my life, but since he's the one who helped me with all of this and accidentally mentioned something to Thea that even he doesn't understand, I'm not sure who else to beg for advice.

He answers on the first ring. "Everything okay, boss man?"

"Can you come back to the greenhouse? Please?"

The line is silent, followed by the jingle of his keys, which filters through the speaker. "Be there in fifteen."

"Drive safe," I say before he hangs up.

True to his word, Colton strolls in exactly fifteen minutes later, his girlfriend, who I've only seen in pictures, in tow. My gaze bounces between the two of them as I try to figure out why he's brought her here.

He points a thumb over his shoulder at her. "This is Magda. Her stepdad is an alien. Figured it was fine to bring her along, due to that fact alone."

My eyebrows jump in surprise. "He is? Which subspecies?" I blink rapidly, forcing myself to focus. "I'm sorry. It's nice to meet you, Magda. I'm Kiran. I should've started with that."

Magda chuckles. "Nice to meet you. And he's a Jëmm'sa. His name is Hamal. Maybe you know him?"

I shake my head. "No. I'm sorry, I don't."

Colton laughs next. "Why are you sorry for not knowing someone? What the hell happened after I left?"

Hands on my hips, I stare up at the ceiling for a few seconds, mulling over the way I can say this without making him feel bad. "Um... You know how you mentioned my love plant to Thea?"

He nods, his eyebrows scrunching.

"Well, I had to tell her the truth. She got mad at me and left, and now I need your help."

"Wait. The love plant really works? I was just kidding around with her. Oh, this is rich. Tell me everything."

I puff out my cheeks with a sigh and then ask, "Are you guys hungry?"

Magda gives me a close-lipped smile. "We were just about to head to dinner when you called, so yes, we are starving."

Head in my hands now, I drum my fingers on my forehead once, then drag them down my face. "I'm fucking everything up tonight."

Both of them race over to me, standing on either side.

"Nonsense," Magda assures me. "It's no big deal. Let's go figure this out, shall we?"

I lead the way to the room where the meal is waiting, and we use the containers to divvy up the food and start eating, and the only time I leave is to grab one more water and check my phone again.

Halfway through our dinner, I've explained the infamous "love plant" to both Magda and Colton, obviously leaving out the transformation part. Colton had no idea that there really was something to the Talahecksiya, confident that when he teased me about it, it was nothing more than a joke.

But now, we have a mess to clean up, and I'm hoping with all I have that these two, who are at a completely different place in their lives, can help me fix everything and win my mate back.

"I think the important thing to remember here, Kiran, is that there'd never really be a good time to reveal something like this to someone like Thea," Magda says.

"Someone like Thea?" I repeat. "What exactly do you mean by that?"

"Well," she starts. "From what you've told me, and what you've told Colton, she's obviously a very independent woman who didn't think she had the time for a relationship. She decides to give it a go and is basically told she's stumbled upon her one and only by randomly visiting a greenhouse and buying a phallus plant one day?" Her eyes widen. "I think it scared her because it seems to me that she was pretty dead set on the single life."

Colton takes Magda's hand and nods at me. "I'd have to agree with Maggie. We have to figure out a way to give her time while also convincing her that this can be a good thing. I mean, what happens to the plant if you guys don't end up together?"

I push my cleared carton away, my gaze flitting between the both of them. "It dies. If she refuses our bond, it will die, and I'll never have another chance to find love again."

CHAPTER TWENTY-FOUR

THEA

Wren drops down onto my couch, holding her bowl of popcorn up in the air to lessen the chance of spillage upon impact.

"Okay, you've made me wait a whole damn week to get the lowdown on Kiran. Why did you cut things off with him?"

I lie back on the chaise beside Wren, staring up at the random black dot that's been on the ceiling since I moved in here ten years ago. And then I tell her everything...

A few crunches later, she asks, "So, you are Kiran's mate, and he knew because you bought that penis plant?"

"Yes, Wren. When you say it like that, you make it sound like a joke, like I'm being overdramatic."

Silence settles between us for so long that I'm forced to break my stare from the ceiling blemish and focus on her.

She shrugs. "Well, is it so bad to know that a plant quite literally led you to your true love? The same true love that made you laugh and screwed you so good that you actually considered giving him a chance? Do you know how many people would give anything for that sort of luck, Thee? Sometimes, people spend their whole lives looking for love."

Of course, she would pull out my nickname to try and soften me a bit... "But I don't need anyone, Wren. I've told you this. I wasn't looking for it."

"Happenstance, Thea. That's the best part of all this. You weren't expecting it. Fate has a way of happening whether you're looking or not. I'm not understanding what's so bad about this."

I drag my hands down my face. "Because he lied to me."

"And if he told you the second you hooked up, that would've been better?"

Why do friends have a way of asking questions you never think of yourself? And why do they always manage to make good fucking points? *Ugh...*

We stare at each other for a moment, Wren searching my face for answers.

"I mean...no. I guess I don't know when would've been a good time to tell me."

She nods. "Exactly. You slept with an alien. You started showing interest in an *alien*. I think it's safe to assume everything about you guys would be far from normal, starting with you bringing home a plant that is an exact replica of Kiran's penis." Her head swivels as she scans the room. "Where is the plant baby, anyway?"

I push up from the couch and make my way to my home office, where I stashed Willy last weekend. Except the state I find the Talahecksiya in has me gasping audibly. Not only are all the leaves of the plant brown around the edges, but Willy's willy has shriveled and shrunk, resembling a dingy, green raisin.

"Willy!" I call, racing for the pot. Steps sound from behind me as I scoop him up.

Wren stands in the doorway, her chest heaving. "What is wrong?"

I hold up the sickly plant. "It's Willy. He's dying!"

"Well, how long has he been in here?"

Once I reach her, she steps aside to let me through the doorway and follows me to the kitchen.

"I shoved him in there last weekend and sort of forgot." Guilt settles in my gut like a boulder. "Quick, can you grab the pepper out of the cupboard?"

The kitchen cupboard slams shut just as I finish adding a couple tablespoons of water. Wren sprinkles the soil with pepper, and I pet the shriveled arm the best I can manage.

"What are you doing?" Wren asks, quiet snickers slipping from her.

I place him up on the sill of my kitchen window so he can get the most light before turning to lean back against the counter. "The third step of caring for Willy is stroking the arm, but since it's, uh—hiding, I had to do my best with what's left."

She nods at me, taking a few steps back from me. "I'm gonna go so you can stroke the plant version of Kiran, but if Willy doesn't recover, I really think you should head back to the greenhouse." Wren slips her jacket on and stands at the door, waiting for me to come over there.

"Why would I do that?"

"Because just like last time, I'm still rooting for Kiran. Besides, what if there's some freaky plant shit that if that plant dies, Kiran's dick falls off or something? Would you want to be responsible for a penis like that ceasing to exist?"

A laugh finally escapes me. "Bye, Wren. Love you."

As I get into bed, Wren's words run through my head... What if something *does* happen to Kiran as a result of what happens to Willy? Could I live with that?

And can I really live without Kiran?

CHAPTER TWENTY-FIVE

KIRAN

Two weeks without my mate feels like how I imagine dying does...

Tonight is my fourteenth night working way past close, and I'm rearranging the dirt and soil room, in desperate need of sweating out whatever these emotions are.

Just as I'm about to put on my headphones, there's a knock on the entrance door. I glance down at my watch, noting that it's well after nine.

"That's weird," I whisper to myself. "Who the hell would be here?"

I huff, guessing it's Colton who forgot something here, or both him and Magda coming to check on me for the third time this week.

Steps from the entrance, the sight through the glass has me frozen in place.

"Thea?"

My brunette goddess stands opposite me, with a familiar plant pot in hand and only a door separating us.

Ever so slowly, I open the door and stare at her as if she's not real. "Hi," I quaver, suddenly unsure of what exactly to say and worried I might scare her away.

She hugs the pot a bit tighter. "Hey."

"Can I help you?" I clear my throat, pulling the door open wider to allow her the space to enter.

She walks by, carefully calculating her steps, then spins to face me. "Are you okay?"

I tilt my head at her, assessing her through squinted eyes. "Is that a loaded question?"

"Well..." She holds up the pot, showing me a shriveled, shrunken, sickly version of my cock. "Willy's dying, and I didn't know if that would have some adverse effect on you or something. So, I had to come and get him fixed. Ya know, to make sure you're okay."

Covering my laugh, I take the plant from her. "I feel like shit, but it has nothing to do with Willy."

Thea's smile is sad. "Why is he dying? I mean, I accidentally locked him in a room alone for about a week, but for the last few days, I've been following the directions on his tag. He's been getting worse."

I'm not prepared to share what I'm about to say, but at the same time, it has to be said. If she's asking, I owe her the truth.

"If you don't accept our mate bond, Willy will die."

She gasps. "And if he dies, what then? You'll grow another Talahecksiya and find another mate?"

As I push the pot across the counter, it makes an ear-piercing screech. "Then my love life dies with it."

"What?"

I sigh, holding my hand out toward Willy. "Every male Cēd'oh receives a *single* Talahecksiya upon reaching adolescence," I explain, holding up one finger. "It's our job to raise it and keep it alive so that one day, it can attract the mate we're destined to spend the rest of our lives with. If our mate refuses the bond, it dies, and that's it."

Thea wrings her hands together, her gaze bouncing between Willy and me. "I don't want Willy to die."

Those words send my heart soaring, but I settle it back down, not wanting to get my hopes up. "It's okay if he does, Thea."

"You'd make that sacrifice for me?"

I shrug. "I'd do anything for you, sweet girl."

Her eyes glaze over at the endearment. "Kiran…"

"Don't, Thea. It's okay. Leave Willy here. I'll take care of everything. Why don't you come back tomorrow and we'll find you a new plant?"

She moves even closer, placing her hand beside mine on the counter. "But I want Willy."

I slump over a smidge. "I can't fix him."

"Well, then it's a good thing that I'm rooting for you, Kiran."

Standing a little taller, I cross my arms over my chest. "Rooting for me?"

Thea nods. "Yeah. I'm rooting for you and for Willy, too. I'm rooting for us."

Movement catches my eye, and as I glance over at the Talahecksiya—*my* Talahecksiya—I notice the brown disappearing from the edges of the leaves, the stems and arm growing again, and the green brightening. "Did you?" I ask.

"Did I what?"

I step closer to my mate, taking her face in my hands. "Accept the bond? Just now?"

"Ummmm…" Her gaze bounces between both of my eyes before landing on a recovering Willy. Then she nods. "Would ya look at that!

I guess I did. I was worried that your penis might shrink and die, just like Willy's."

A guffaw bursts out of me. "I assure you, my dick is just fine."

"Prove it," she orders.

Thea squeals as I bend down to grab her ass and lift her up. She wraps herself around me, her mouth hovering just within reach of mine.

"With pleasure, my mate."

Wasting no time, I reach my office and shut the door behind us. Then I swipe everything off of my desk and set her down, boxing her in between my arms.

"Unbutton my pants, sweet girl. Pull it out and see for yourself."

Thea gets to work, pushing my pants down to free me from the material. Wrapping her hand around my cock, she strokes me once before locking eyes with me. "Got any pepper?"

THE END

EPILOGUE

One year later...

THEA

"I still can't believe we were able to fit all of your things in this tiny-ass moving truck." Kiran marvels at the small truck. "You really managed to sell everything else?"

I place a hand over his bulging, sweaty bicep as he holds up my office desk like it weighs no more than a feather. "Yep! I didn't need it, Kiran. I love all the furnishings in your house way more."

He smirks, flexing his arm even harder. "Why, thank you, babe. And what about the mover? Do you like him, too?"

"Is that what you're calling yourself now?" I chuckle.

His dimples pop as his smirk morphs into a full-toothed grin. "Indeed. I am moving your shit. Hence the term, 'mover.'"

Nodding along with his thoughts, I lean back against the truck and begin unzipping my sweatshirt, unveiling a brand-new, very lacy bra.

It may be March in Michigan, but it's warmer than average today, and we're both sweating our asses off from moving me into Kiran's house. He agreed to a year of dating before cohabitating, which gave me more than enough time to come up with a business plan and sell all the things from my house that I didn't need in order to finally prepare to start up my dream business of owning a restaurant that serves everything flight style and begin another chapter of our life.

I shoot him a wink. "What do you think?"

"I think that, one: you're very lucky we have no nearby neighbors, and two: you're the sexiest woman I've ever laid eyes on." Kiran's emerald gaze travels up and down my body, admiring every inch, not just the bra. That's what I love most about him—he's in love with every version of me, even the sweatpants-wearing, too-independent-to-move-in-with-her-fated-mate-right-away me.

As he makes his way up the stairs to the house with a grunt that has goosebumps erupting over my skin, I wonder if this is his way of telling me he wants to get the moving portion of our day done before we get to the good stuff. This is my first time living with a man—let alone an alien—and I look forward to learning the ropes of cohabitation with Kiran.

Kiran stalks back out to me, halfway through his transformation, and eyes glowing bright with hunger. A growl escapes his lips, and I have to fight down a swallow over the sudden pressure in my throat at the sight.

A predator stalking his prey; that's exactly what he is at this moment, and it sends a thrill through my nether regions.

Closing in, he boxes me in against the truck. Then he slowly drops to his knees, taking a long, slow inhale during his descent, his stare locked on mine the entire time.

His head stops at my chest, where he playfully bites at my pebbled nipples through the lacy fabric, pulling a desperate moan from me.

"Good girl," he murmurs against my skin. "You're always so ready, even out here in the cool air."

I can't even focus on what he's saying, because he already had me at "good girl." Isn't this what fantasies are made of? Yes. I think so.

Moving to stand, Kiran throws me over his shoulder.

"Kiran! What the hell do you think you're doing?" I give his ass a light pinch, to which he laughs.

My body bounces with each of his steps as he walks back into his—well, now *our*—house and heads for the bathroom. "We're much too sweaty, Thea. I think a shower is in order, don't you?"

"Definitely," I respond, already licking my lips in anticipation.

Without removing our clothes, he steps into the ginormous, glass, walk-in shower and turns the water on so it pelts us from all angles, due to the multiple shower heads hanging at various heights.

I squeal as the chilly water soaks me. "It's cold!"

He chuckles, ridding me of the now-soaked clothing covering my lower half as the temperature slowly warms. The way he's able to do that one-handed, without letting me slip an inch, has me biting my lip. Kiran is so fucking hot, and he's all mine. I will get to spend the rest of my days like this, and I can't wait.

Once he has the lower part of me bare, I get to work on maneuvering my sweatshirt off, which is a bit hard seeing as I'm still mostly upside down.

Kiran slaps my ass, and I yelp. "What was that for?"

"Your ass looks good, and I was giving you a warning."

"For what?"

He pulls my legs down a bit so that I'm at least upright before pushing me up against the shower wall. "Wanted to distract you from taking that bra off."

I raise my eyebrows at him, and pride swells in my belly. Apparently, my shopping trip was a success.

But then Kiran maneuvers his arms, one at a time, until they're between my legs and cupping my ass, where he then pushes up on my behind until he sets me on his shoulders with his face to my core. I've never been more grateful for tall ceilings.

I gulp. "Noted. But we have a problem."

He kisses my lower belly. "What's that, my love?"

"You're still very much dressed."

"Don't you worry about that," he mumbles against my skin before pressing his textured tongue to my aching bud, gently rubbing it side to side. "Tilt that showerhead so it's spraying on those gorgeous tits, sweet girl."

I reach up, trying not to pull the whole damn thing off the wall, but I'm so consumed in pleasure, it's hard to concentrate. Somehow, I manage the job, sending rivulets of warmth over my chest, down my belly, and between where my core and Kiran's mouth meet.

My grasp moves to his hair, running through and pulling on the strands as Kiran laps at me with pristine focus, bringing me closer and closer to release.

Kiran raises his forearms—keeping my thighs secured in the crook of his elbows—and grabs onto my breasts, placing a thumb to each of my nipples and working them in circles. It's addicting—the combined texture of both his now-fully-transformed thumb pads and the wet lace of my bra. Between that and the roots at the tip of his tongue working either side of my clit, I'm at the edge and falling over a second later in yet another powerful orgasm gifted to me by my fated alien mate.

"Kiran! Oh! Fuck, *yesssssss!*" I scream, convulsing in his hold so much that the wet sound of my skin sticking to and peeling away from the damp shower wall echoes around us.

I'm not given much time before Kiran is pulling me down and placing me on my feet before him. I try not to let my wobbly legs send me crashing to the shower floor.

Lifting my chin with his pointer finger, he draws my face to his. "On your knees, Thea. And give me your bra."

KIRAN

With Thea's essence on my tongue, her perfect, naked body kneeling before me, and her wet bra in my hand, I make quick work of the showerheads, tilting them all so the water continues to keep us warm but doesn't drown us in the process.

Two steps back is all it takes for the back of my knees to hit the built-in bench. I rid myself of my soaked, heavy clothing and take a seat, my hard cock standing at attention.

My mate loves me in my humanoid form, but a feral look grows in her eyes every time I'm fully transformed.

Her heavy-lidded stare scans me from head to toe before landing on my dick. She licks her lips as she waits for what comes next.

She settles back to relax on her heels. "What are we doing, Kiran?"

Taking her bra, I wrap it around my shaft—not too tight—and slowly move it up and down with my hand, playing with myself while Thea watches.

A sharp gasp permeates the air.

"Touch yourself, sweet girl."

Thea spreads her knees apart and uses one hand to grab onto her breast while the other travels down, down, down to her center. Using two fingers, she rubs her clit, gently rocking forward and backward.

The sight has me bucking up into my hand, envisioning what it will feel like when I have her riding me in a few moments.

"Mmm," I moan. "You are perfect, baby. Absolutely perfect. Does that feel good?"

She nods. "So good. But Kiran..."

"Hmm?"

"I want you inside me. Please." Soft mewls spill from her lips until I can't take it anymore.

Tossing the bra to the shower floor, I call her over with a crook of my finger. "Ride me, Thea. Show me how much you want me inside you."

My large hands wrap around her waist to steady her as she climbs into my lap and lowers herself onto my cock. Moans escape from both of our mouths as our bodies adjust and slowly begin to move with each other.

Nothing compares to making love with your person. I don't think I could ever find a way to encapsulate what it feels like; not at all.

With euphoria on the very nearby precipice, I find myself unable to fight the words I've waited to say since getting this amazing woman to move in with me.

"Marry me, Thea?" I ask.

Her eyes widen, and her movements slow but never stop. "What?"

"Marry me. Please. Spend the rest of your days exploring life, fighting over the best ice cream flavor, and falling deeper in love with me. Never stop, my mate. Accept fate with me."

Warmth swims through my stomach as she wraps her arms around my neck and picks up her pace. I pull her to me, my breathing growing heavier as I anxiously await her answer.

"Yes." She kisses me. "A trillion times, yes. I'll marry you, Kiran. Of course, I will."

A smile so large, it actually hurts as it pulls up on the corners of my mouth, breaks free. "Good, my mate. Because I've dreamt of this since the day you strolled into my greenhouse, and I'll never stop dreaming about us and our future. Not ever." I reach up and rip a root from the top of my head, quickly tying it in a circle as we sit here, still connected with one another.

Placing it on her ring finger, I look deep into her eyes and promise, "Just for now, okay?"

"It's perfect," she responds, smashing her mouth to mine once more.

We move faster and faster with each other, chasing the only feeling that could possibly come close to ever comparing to what it feels like to find the one and have them agree to marry you.

And as we fall over the edge together, there's one thing I know that's for certain. Holding her gorgeous face between my hands, I say, "I've been rooting for you before I ever knew you, Thea. I love you."

Tears well in her eyes, enhancing her crystal-blue irises. "I love you, too."

ACKNOWLEDGMENTS

I'm not even sure where to begin... The amount of people I've been blessed to know, meet, and feel supported and loved by is infinite. I know for a fact that if I were to name everyone, I'd still find a way to unintentionally miss someone, and I never EVER want to do that. So, I'll try to keep this brief and all-encompassing.

My family: Some of you may not be big fans of a spicy book like this, but I still appreciate the support and excitement anyway. All of you know that nothing is going to stop me when I put my mind to something, so in a way, thanks for making room while I march to the beat of my own drum. I hope that with this story, I'm showing some of you that it's okay to take chances, even if you're unsure of the reactions you'll receive from those closest to you. Either way, thank you for believing in me. I'd be lost without you.

My friends: I'm not sure what I ever did in my life or past lives to deserve all of you, but I'm beyond lucky. BEYOND. There are NO words that will ever be able to summarize how much I truly love all of you. Thank you for sticking by my side all of these years, for giving me grace when I need it, and for always being so supportive and amazing. I know the world is jealous of the crew I have, and they should be. They really should be.

M²: I'm not going to go into detail about why you're listed in here, because you already know the reason. But just know that I'm thankful to know you. Thanks for the inspiration. ;)

My CPs: When I posted in those writing groups searching for critique partners, I never imagined what all three of you would come to mean to me. I'm one of the lucky ones—to call you friends, to call you critique partners, to read your amazing works, and just to know you. You're some of the kindest, humblest, perfect human beings, and your writing deserves ALL the recognition. My books wouldn't become what they are without you.

My editor, Andrea: Thank you for taking a last-minute chance on me with this book. Thank you for loving the story and the characters as much as you did. I know for a fact that I couldn't have pulled this book together, nor could I have made it what it is today, without you. So, thank you. You're truly one of the best! Oh, and tell your husband that I stare at the fanart he made me at least once a day! ;)

My cover designer, Victoria: To put this plainly, YOU KNOCKED THIS COVER OUT OF THE FRIGGIN' PARK. I'm still on cloud nine when I look at it. You have created the version of Kiran I've been dreaming about in my mind. Thank you SO much for taking this project on at the last minute and for creating my dream cover. I'm truly appreciative.

Pen Pals: You all know who you are. I think it's important to mention that even when I was really struggling those few months and super absent in our group chat, your hard work and determination with your craft continued to inspire me. I knew that when I was feeling better, I was going to be able to do this because you all continue to do it every single day, even when it's hard. Thank you for being my writing friends, and thank you for the amazing community we've created together. I'm lucky to have wound up there with all of you.

My readers: As many of you already know, this writing journey wouldn't even be possible without you. Whether this is your first time reading something by me or not, I'm immensely grateful for you. Thank you for taking a chance on something I worked so hard on, something that's so near and dear to me, and a story I hope will make you laugh. That was the goal with this book. I could never thank you enough for the numerous ways you support my writing career. It means more than you could ever imagine. If you ever need a safe person, you know where to find me online.

To my dog, Finnick: No one will ever know the parts of me and my life that you do. I'm lucky to not only have a creature who looks at me and loves me so meaningfully—even though I feel so undeserving at times—but also to always have someone by my side on the late nights of writing, to listen to my incessant idea babbling, and to comfort me when I am struggling to just *do*. You make life worth living. Thank you for being my reason to wake up every morning.

And finally, anyone and everyone in between: As I'm sure you can probably tell, I could make a list a mile long of people to thank for these things, and I'd still find more to thank. Like the formatting company I was able to format my book with, or the café employee who smiled at me when I was struggling to find words... The list is endless. So, to anyone who has impacted my life, my writing, or my journey in some way—thank you. I'll never stop being thankful, because I'm beyond lucky to have discovered what makes me truly happy, and I'll never stop fighting for that. I'll never stop fighting for the survival of stories and art in a world plagued by people who hope to snuff out the creativity we all need to thrive and survive. **Never.**

Thank you for taking a chance on me. It means the world. I owe my success to you.

XOXO,

Meghan

AUTHOR BIO

Meghan Monarch is a romance author writing flutter-worthy love stories in various romance sub-genres. She loves athleisure wear, movie theaters, dancing in grocery store aisles, obsessing over her favorite fandoms, loud music, and even louder laughter.

She writes from her Michigan home, where she lives with her dog, Finnick—a super cool standard poodle with a colored mohawk.

When she's not writing, she's reading, working out, relaxing, or going out on solo dates and spending time with her favorite people.

Check out her website and follow her on social media to stay notified of news and updates.

www.meghanmonarch.com

www.ingramcontent.com/pod-product-compliance
Lightning Source LLC
Chambersburg PA
CBHW071431300726
48976CB00004B/1297